MAIN

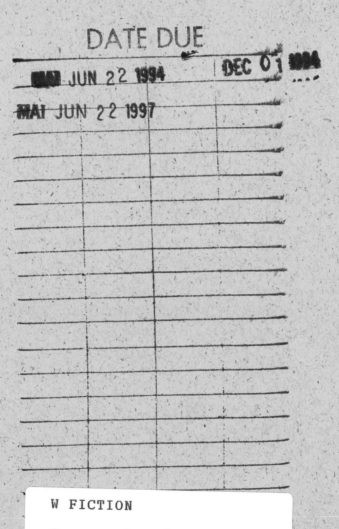

DATE DUE

MAY JUN 22 1994	DEC 01 1994
MAY JUN 22 1997	

The Best Western Stories of
ED GORMAN

The Western Writers Series is edited
by Bill Pronzini and Martin H. Greenberg

The Best Western Stories of

ED GORMAN

EDITED BY BILL PRONZINI

AND MARTIN H. GREENBERG

SWALLOW PRESS

OHIO UNIVERSITY PRESS

ATHENS

Introduction copyright © 1992 by
Bill Pronzini

Swallow Press/Ohio University Press
books are printed on acid-free paper. ♾

Printed in the United States of America.
All rights reserved.

Library of Congress Cataloging-in-Publication Data

Gorman, Edward.
  The best western stories of Ed Gorman / edited by Bill Pronzini
and Martin H. Greenberg.
      p.   cm. — (The Western writers series)
  Includes bibliographical references.
  ISBN 0-8040-0959-7
  1. Western stories.   I. Pronzini, Bill.   II. Greenberg, Martin
Harry.   III. Title.   IV. Series: Western writers series (Carbondale,
Ill.)
PS3557.O759A6   1992
813′.54—dc20   92-15421
                                                                      CIP
                                                                       AC

Designed by Laury A. Egan

For Ben Johnson—
A far better stepson
than I deserve.

Contents

Acknowledgments

Introduction

A Renaissance Writer: Ed Gorman

BY BILL PRONZINI

In an age of literary specialization, Ed Gorman is surely a renaissance writer.

Most professionals today concentrate on one particular category or type of fiction or nonfiction, e.g., the crime story; perhaps go a step further and concentrate on a particular sub-genre, e.g., the series detective story. One reason for such specialization is the limited number of available markets, especially for short fiction. Another reason is that, theoretically, at least, the writer avoids the pitfall of spreading himself too thin; hones his craft in effect by repetition—writes the same sort of thing over and over until he perfects it.

Ed Gorman does not subscribe to this literary philosophy. There is too much danger, in his opinion, of stagnation; of familiarity breeding burnout or complacency; of the fine edge of one's abilities being unconsciously dulled rather than sharpened. The challenge of working on something new and different is what helps keep his interest keen and what allows him to stretch his talent to its limits.

In but a single decade, Gorman has donned a remarkable number of literary hats; tried his hand at nearly every type of modern fiction and nonfiction, working under his own byline and several pseudonyms. And he has done all of this with an impressively high rate of success.

He has written western novels and short stories. Historical novels about his native Cedar Rapids. Literary short stories. Series detective fiction. Mainstream suspense novels. Adventure novels. Horror fiction. Fantasy and science fiction. Erotica. Continuity for comic books and graphic arts publications.

In collaboration with Max Allan Collins, he is the author of a critical biography of *noir* novelist Jim Thompson, *The Killers Inside Him* (1983).

He has ghosted two bestselling books on occult themes.

He has written numerous essays, how-to articles, nostalgia sketches, and other short works of nonfiction.

He is an accomplished book reviewer; his column "A Closer Look," has run for many years in the Cedar Rapids *Gazette*.

He is a critically acclaimed anthologist. *Westeryear* (1988) is one of the most satisfying western anthologies of recent years; and such volumes as *The Black Lizard Anthology of Crime Fiction* (1987) and *Dark Crimes* (1991) have earned him a reputation as today's premier compiler of *noir* short fiction.

He is co-founder (with Robert J. Randisi), co-publisher (with Martin H. Greenberg), and editor of *Mystery Scene*, an important magazine devoted to news, features, reviews of and commentary about contemporary crime fiction.

With Martin Greenberg, he is co-editor of a line of reprints of neo-classic mystery and detective novels published under the "Mystery Scene" aegis by Carroll & Graf.

And he is co-editor (again with Martin Greenberg) of Mystery Scene Press, a line of single-author collections of crime fiction published in affiliation with Pulphouse Publishing of Eugene, Oregon.

Few writers working in the eighties and nineties can match Gorman's ambitious productivity. None can match the diversity of his accomplishments.

Ed Gorman was born in Cedar Rapids, Iowa, on November 29, 1941, first son of Edward and Bernadine Gorman. His early education was in Catholic schools in Cedar Rapids; from 1962 to 1965 he attended Coe College where he majored in English. After leaving college, he worked for fifteen years as a writer-director of TV commercials, in other advertising-related jobs, and briefly as a political speechwriter. In 1980 he founded a small advertising agency in Cedar Rapids, which he ran successfully until 1988, when he sold it to devote himself entirely to freelance writing, editing, and publishing.

Gorman began writing for publication in the mid-sixties, and made his first sale to a men's magazine in 1966. His book reviews began appearing in the Cedar Rapids *Gazette* in 1975, but his production of fiction and other types of nonfiction remained sporadic until after his marriage to Carol Maxwell, a successful writer of young-adult books, in 1982. The acceptance of his first mystery novel, *Rough Cut*, by St. Martin's Press in 1984 opened the floodgates.

Mysteries—or, more properly, crime fiction—comprise the largest percentage of Gorman's output. (Crime and dark-mystery or *noir* elements are also prevalent in his other fiction, including his westerns.) Written in a lean, deliberately rough-edged style, his contemporary detective and suspense stories are an amalgam of pure entertainment, social commentary, symbolic statement, and in-depth studies of what Gorman terms "outsiders trying to make their peace with the world." They are also largely autobiographical. "Each book," he has said, "deals with some aspect of my life, either in terms of background—the advertising industry, for example—or in terms of theme. One is about the aftermath of a divorce; another about coming to terms with alcoholism."

Like *Rough Cut*, his second mystery novel, *New, Improved Murder* (1985) is set in the often cutthroat world of advertising; it also introduced Jack Dwyer, the first of Gorman's three series detectives and a quintessential outsider. Dwyer, an ex-cop, part-time actor, security guard, and blue-collar philosopher, has appeared in five subsequent novels, notably *The Autumn Dead* (1988) in which he is drawn to a former lover and, through her, into violence and a confrontation with his past that profoundly changes him. (Gorman considers *The Autumn Dead* his best novel; has expressed the hope that his son—who is now in his twenties—will read it again at age sixty and "have an epiphany of sorts and say, 'So that's what my old man was all about.'") If any criticism can be leveled against the Dwyer novels, it is that the city in which they take place is unnamed (although by implication it is Cedar Rapids). This amorphousness of locale robs them of an extra measure of reality that they might otherwise have had.

Gorman's second private detective protagonist, Jack Walsh, is likewise a social misfit—a man in his fifties, scarred by the death of his partner, in love with a much younger woman. Walsh operates out of a fully organized Cedar Rapids milieu and is an even more complex individual than Dwyer, with ties to the past that color his dealings with the present and his attitude toward the future. Walsh's book-length debut, *The Night Remembers* (1991), is the most emotionally charged of the author's crime novels—so much so that the mystery, even though it focuses on a major topical theme, is subordinate throughout to Walsh's agonized concern with his young woman friend's probable cancer and the fate of her (and perhaps his) infant son.

A third series detective, Tobin, a five-foot-five-inch movie critic with an explosive temper, appears in two novels, *Murder on the Aisle* (1987) and *Several Deaths Later* (1988). Both contain much that is insightful and thought-provoking, but they do not represent the cutting edge of Gorman's work.

A nonseries suspense novel that does represent the cutting edge is *Night Kills* (1991). Its background combination of advertising and the dark and deadly teenage-runaway underground makes it a *noir* thriller that captures all too well the attitudes and tenor of the nineties.

Also of major importance in the Gorman crime-fiction ouevre are such short stories as "Turn Away," an evocative Dwyer which was the recipient of a Shamus Award from the Private Eye Writers of America for best short story of 1987; and "Prisoners," a frighteningly topical tale of a family gathering behind prison walls, which was nominated for a Mystery Writers of America Edgar in 1991.

Of Gorman's other fiction, noteworthy are his psychological horror novels as by Daniel Ransom (which he dismisses as "B-movies in print form," though the best of them—*The Forsaken* (1988) and *The Long Midnight* (1992)—are much better than that assessment); and a collection of primarily dark-suspense short fiction, *Prisoners and Other Stories* (1992).

The western and historical fiction of Ed Gorman is individualized by the same *noir* qualities as his contemporary crime and horror fiction; peopled by the same sort of out-of-the-mainstream characters. When he is dealing with Cedar Rapids in the 1800s and 1890s, as he does in two novels, the background is historically accurate and the stories generally upbeat in nature. His westerns, which are anything but traditional, are much bleaker in tone and content, and take place on lonely, tragic, mythical landscapes. Gorman believes strongly in perpetuating the western myth created by hundreds of writers and filmmakers throughout this century. He quotes

Rouben Mamoulian: "What survives best is myth. Realism dies." And he has said in an interview, "While writers such as Larry McMurtry and Loren Estleman have produced fine novels that balance history and prose-poetry, too many so-called historicals are just term papers with dialogue. If I want history, leave me to my history books. If I want entertainment, leave me to my myths."

It is no surprise, then, that his most intriguing character is Leo Guild, an 1890s lawman-turned-bounty hunter who operates in what is nominally referred to as the Dakota Territory, but which in fact (and in spite of his comments in his essay, "Writing the Modern Western") is a shadowland, a kind of western Twilight Zone. Guild is a more dour, more tormented, frontier version of Jack Walsh: fifty-odd, constantly in need of money, riddled with guilt over an accident in which he shot and killed a six-year-old girl. His guilt is both a leitmotif and a force that drives him through each of his adventures, giving him often painful insights into the people he meets, leading him to question many of the values he once took for granted.

(The guilt felt by others, for various reasons, is also a recurring theme in the series; as are love, revenge, greed, obsession, dissociation and loneliness. Morality plays, allegories, Grecian tragedies . . . these are the stuff of Gorman's often nightmarish vision of frontier America.)

Guild (1987) is the first and least ambitious book in the saga, in which Guild helps two women, a bereaved young Swede named Annie and a strong-minded newspaper editor, Ruby Gillespie, by breaking the vicious stranglehold of banker Frank Cord on a small town. Much more visceral and successful is *Death Ground* (1988), about which Gorman has this to say:

> I wanted to write about a violent man who discovers, when it's too late, his capacity for love. So I came up with

Kriker [a crazed, gun-wielding mountain man], whom I based on a boyhood friend of mine who ended up in prison at seventeen for cutting a gas-station attendent in half with a sawed-off shotgun. I also wanted to take the Graham Greeneian notion of a priest who is also an atheist and bring him and Kriker together with Guild against a backdrop of nature at its worst . . . [My wife] feels that *Death Ground*'s ultimate theme is redemption and she's probably right.

In the third Guild book, *Blood Game,* the grim and violent world of bareknuckle prizefighting is the background for a tale of greed, duplicity, and obsession. About this novel, Gorman says that his dual purpose was to put Guild into a situation where "he is forced, by economic necessity, to work at something he personally finds repugnant; [and to] say something about racism in our country, a subject that inevitably comes up when boxing is discussed, especially turn-of-the-century boxing when a black man risked his life just by stepping into the ring with a white man. Black boxers regularly received death threats from anonymous crowd members."

Dark Trail (1991) is the bleakest of the Guild novels. When he crosses paths with his former wife Sarah, who left him years earlier for gunfighter Frank Evans, she tells him Evans has recently left her for a younger woman named Beth; she desperately wants Evans back and begs Guild to help her. One complication is that Beth's former lover, another gunman, Ben Rittenauer, has sworn to kill Evans; a second complication is that a rich and powerful man, Adair, has invited both gunfighters to his ranch for a birthday celebration, the main attraction of which will be a shootout between the two—the winner to get ten thousand dollars and Beth. These components lead to bitter tragedy for all concerned.

While there is violence in the Guild series, it is secondary—as is everything else including plot—to character development. People are Gorman's primary concern: who they are, why they do what they do, the consequences of their actions upon themselves and others. None of his male characters are the larger-than-life heroes and villains found in so much western fiction. Nor are any of his women of the plucky or brazen or haughty or stand-tall-beside-her-man ilk. All of his characters, of both sexes, are nonstereotypically human: some good, some evil, but most a combination of both in varying degrees; vulnerable, petty, brave, cowardly, riddled with self doubts and secret longings; trying the best way they can to survive in difficult circumstances. (He is particularly adept at portraying the "soiled dove" as she must have been; Lucy in the story "Deathman" is one example.) Emotions run high throughout each novel; they are what propel the narrative. And yet Gorman's prose is the antithesis of emotional—hard, spare, almost Hemingwayesque in its reliance on dialogue to achieve the author's desired effects.

The Guild novels have been described by different reviewers as "westerns for grown-ups" and "westerns for those who don't like reading westerns." On the one hand, these statements are true enough. On the other hand, they are misleading. In point of fact the Guild books are not westerns at all, in any except a superficial way. They are parables—set-piece excursions into a mythical, mystical realm where the people are real but everything else is phantasm and shadow. In this sense, they are the true distilled essence of *noir* fiction.

The same is true of a nonseries novel, *What the Dead Men Say* (1990), even though its stated setting is Iowa in 1898. When merchant Septemus Ryan's young daughter is killed during a bank robbery, he literally goes out of his mind with grief—becomes obsessed with finding and destroying the three men responsible. It takes him years to identify the men, and when he does it is by accident in the town of Myles, where he has come with his sheltered, sixteen-year-old nephew, James Hogan, for an agricultural fair. James is witness to his uncle's deepening descent into madness, and the ultimate effect on him is thunderously profound. The publisher's dust jacket blurb describes the novel as "a taut, powerful tale of grief and vengeance, and coming of age." It is that, but it is also existential, almost nihilistic in its depiction of the futility not only of revenge but of other human pursuits, for all of the principal characters become victims of one kind or another and there is little left for the survivors except hopelessness and despair. Reading *What the Dead Men Say* is a gut-wrenching experience not every reader will want to undergo; but those who do will not soon forget it.

Much more pleasant fare are a recent pseudonymous western—*Ride into Yesterday,* as by Christopher Keegan—and Gorman's two historicals. The Keegan novel, about a man named Payne who sets out to investigate the alleged suicide by hanging of his brother, is played out on the same sort of shadowy landscape as the Guild novels; but the shadows here are not nearly as dark, and the story, for all its psychological impact, is more closely allied to the traditional western than any of Gorman's other novels. *Graves' Retreat* (1989) takes place in Cedar Rapids in 1884 and mixes authentic early baseball lore with mystery, romance, and bank robbery. The hero ("the only true-blue hero I've ever written about," Gorman says) is a former baseball pitcher turned bank teller, Les Graves, who tries to help his brother T.Z. escape the influence of an outlaw, Neely, and who winds up in a great deal of trouble for his pains. *Night of Shadows* (1990) is a fact-based portrait of Anna Tolan, Cedar Rapids' first uniformed policewoman. The time here is 1895, when the only position open to a woman on the city's police force is as a matron; Anna is determined to change that, and succeeds when she is given the plum assignment of shepherding a notorious (and alcoholic) gunslinger in and out of town without incident. A psychopathic murderer, his equally terrifying mother, and "newfangled detection methods" also play major roles in the narrative.

Gorman's western and historical short stories are every bit as unusual and provocative as his novels, utilizing a few of the same themes as well as others that are markedly different. Some of the stories take place in his western Twilight Zone; others have authentic backgrounds and settings—the Civil War, northern Montana, Cedar Rapids in 1890, Los Angeles in the early years of this century, the Midwest in the present day. Only one is what may be termed a traditional western story, and that only by stretching the definition.

Arguably, "The Face" is Gorman's finest short story of any type—perhaps his single best piece of fiction. Set on a Civil War battlefield, it concerns a young doctor, a battle-hardened Confederate general, and a mortally wounded young soldier with a face quite unlike any other man's. In many ways it is a perfect allegory for our times; and its ending—and its message—has haunted this reader for months.

"Gunslinger" tells of a Missouri farmer on a mission of vengeance in the days when Hollywood filmmaking was in its infancy; famed silent film director Thomas Ince is one of its characters. An O. Henry twist gives the title special meaning.

"Guild and the Indian Woman" is the only short story to date featuring Leo Guild. First published in Gorman's *Westeryear* anthology, it deals with a frontier doctor, the doctor's son, a tribe of Indians, and two distinctly different kinds of murder. In setting, theme, and understated emotional content it is typical of the Guild series.

"Mainwaring's Gift" is a Christmas story. In the hands of a lesser writer, its subject matter might have been developed into a mawkishly sentimental tale; in Gorman's hands it is an offbeat and moving celebration of the Yuletide spirit.

The one story in these pages closest to a traditional western is "Blood Truth." What is traditional is the central idea of a Montana bounty hunter bringing in a prisoner; what is non-traditional is the outcome of a night they spend at the isolated home of the prisoner's mother.

Brief though it is, "Dance Girl" is reminiscent of *What the Dead Men Say* in its grim, existential depiction of murder, revenge, and sudden truth in old Cedar Rapids.

The shadowland of Leo Guild is the setting for "Deathman," the chilling and memorable tale of a professional hangman named Hawes, a prostitute named Lucy, and a terrible secret buried deep—but not deep enough—in a man's psyche.

"Love and Trooper Hook" brings together a pudgy, twenty-three-year-old U.S. Cavalry recruit, the nineteen-year-old daughter of his company's captain, and a valley full of rattle-snakes, with poignant results.

The time frame of the original novelette, "Pards," is the present, the setting the Midwest, the story that of two men—Bromley, a failed middle-aged writer with an abiding passion for the western films of his youth; and Rex Stone, the aging cowboy star he reveres—and of what happens when they meet face to face. Deceptively simple in the telling and in its denouement, it offers more than one thematic statement for the thoughtful reader to consider.

The final two selections are a pair of brief nonfiction pieces—a nostalgic look at Roy Rogers and his films, which perhaps inspired "Pards"; and "Writing the Modern Western," in which Gorman shares his views on western fiction and reveals how he came to write the Guild series.

Enter, now, the worlds—real and twilight—of Ed Gorman. They aren't always pleasant places in which to dwell; but they are invariably interesting, stimulating, and quite extraordinary places to visit.

The Face

THE WAR WAS going badly. In the past month more than sixty men had disgraced the Confederacy by deserting, and now the order was to shoot deserters on sight. This was in other camps and other regiments. Fortunately, none of our men had deserted at all.

As a young doctor, I knew even better than our leaders just how hopeless our war had become. The public knew General Lee had been forced to cross the Potomac with ten thousand men who lacked shoes, hats and who at night had to sleep on the ground without blankets. But I knew—in the first six months in this post—that our men suffered from influenza, diphtheria, smallpox, yellow fever and even cholera; ravages from which they would never recover; ravages more costly than bullets and the advancing armies of the Yankees. Worse, because toilet and bathing facilities were practically nil, virtually every man suffered from tics and mites and many suffered from scurvy, their bodies on fire. Occasionally, you would see a man go mad, do crazed dances in the moonlight trying to get the bugs off him. Soon enough he would be dead.

This was the war in the spring and while I have here referred to our troops as "men," in fact they were mostly boys, some as young as thirteen. In the night, freezing and sometimes wounded, they cried out for their mothers, and it was not uncommon to hear one or two of them sob while they prayed aloud.

I tell you this so you will have some idea of how horrible

things had become for our beloved Confederacy. But even given the suffering and madness and despair I'd seen for the past two years as a military doctor, nothing had prepared me for the appearance of the Virginia man in our midst.

On the day he was brought in on a buckboard, I was working with some troops, teaching them how to garden. If we did not get vegetables and fruit into our diets soon, all of us would have scurvy. I also appreciated the respite that working in the warm sun gave me from surgery. In the past week alone, I'd amputated three legs, two arms and numerous hands and fingers. None had gone well, conditions were so filthy.

Every amputation had ended in death except one and this man—boy; he was fourteen—pleaded with me to kill him every time I checked on him. He'd suffered a head wound and I'd had to relieve the pressure by trepanning into his skull. Beneath the blood and pus in the hole I'd dug, I could see his brain squirming. There was no anesthetic, of course, except whiskey and that provided little comfort against the violence of my bone saw. It was one of those periods when I could not get the tart odor of blood from my nostrils, nor its feel from my skin. Sometimes, standing at the surgery table, my boots would become soaked with it and I would squish around in them all day.

The buckboard was parked in front of the General's tent. The driver jumped down, ground-tied the horses, and went quickly inside.

He returned a few moments later with General Sullivan, the commander. Three men in familiar gray uniforms followed the General.

The entourage walked around to the rear of the wagon. The driver, an enlisted man, pointed to something in the buckboard. The General, a fleshy, bald man of fifty-some years, leaned over the wagon and peered downward.

Quickly, the General's head snapped back and then his

whole body followed. It was as if he'd been stung by something coiled and waiting for him in the buckboard.

The General shook his head and said, "I want this man's entire face covered. Especially his face."

"But, General," the driver said. "He's not dead. We shouldn't cover his face."

"You heard what I said!" General Sullivan snapped. And with that, he strutted back into his tent, his men following.

I was curious, of course, about the man in the back of the wagon. I wondered what could have made the General start the way he had. He'd looked almost frightened.

I wasn't to know till later that night.

My rounds made me late for dinner in the vast tent used for the officers' mess. I always felt badly about the inequity of officers having beef stew while the men had, at best, hardtack and salt pork. Not so bad that I refused to eat it, of course, which made me feel hypocritical on top of being sorry for the enlisted men.

Not once in my time here had I ever dined with General Sullivan. I was told on my first day here that the General, an extremely superstitious man, considered doctors bad luck. Many people feel this way. Befriend a doctor and you'll soon enough find need of his services.

So I was surprised when General Sullivan, carrying a cup of steaming coffee in a huge, battered tin cup, sat down across from the table where I ate alone, my usual companions long ago gone back to their duties.

"Good evening, Doctor."

"Good evening, General."

"A little warmer tonight."

"Yes."

He smiled dourly. "Something's got to go our way, I suppose."

I returned his smile. "I suppose." I felt like a child trying to act properly for the sake of an adult. The General frightened me.

The General took out a stogie, clipped off the end, sniffed it, licked it, then put it between his lips and fired it. He did all this with a ritualistic satisfaction that made me think of better times in my home city of Charleston, of my father and uncles handling their smoking in just the same way.

"A man was brought into camp this afternoon," he said.

"Yes," I said. "In a buckboard."

He eyed me suspiciously. "You've seen him up close?"

"No. I just saw him delivered to your tent." I had to be careful of how I put my next statement. I did not want the General to think I was challenging his reasoning. "I'm told he was not taken to any of the hospital tents."

"No, he wasn't." The General wasn't going to help me.

"I'm told he was put under quarantine in a tent of his own."

"Yes."

"May I ask why?"

He blew two plump white perfect rings of smoke toward the ceiling. "Go have a look at him, then join me in my tent."

"You're afraid he may have some contagious disease?"

The General considered the length of his cigar. "Just go have a look at him, Doctor. Then we'll talk."

With that, the General stood up, his familiar brusque self once again, and was gone.

The guard set down his rifle when he saw me. "Good evenin', Doctor."

"Good evening."

He nodded to the tent behind him. "You seen him yet?"

"No; not yet."

He was young. He shook his head. "Never seen anything like it. Neither has the priest. He's in there with him now." In the chill, crimson dusk I tried to get a look at the guard's face. I

couldn't. My only clue to his mood was the tone of his voice—
one of great sorrow.

I lifted the tent flap and went in.

A lamp guttered in the far corner of the small tent, casting huge and playful shadows across the walls. A hospital
cot took up most of the space. A man's body lay beneath the
covers. A sheer cloth had been draped across his face. You
could see it billowing with the man's faint breath. Next to
the cot stood Father Lynott. He was silver-haired and chunky.
His black cassock showed months of dust and grime. Like
most of us, he was rarely able to get hot water for necessi-
ties.

At first, he didn't seem to hear me. He stood over the cot
torturing black rosary beads through his fingers. He stared
directly down at the cloth draped on the man's face.

Only when I stood next to him did Father Lynott look up.
"Good evening, Father."

"Good evening, Doctor."

"The General wanted me to look at this man."

He stared at me. "You haven't seen him, then?"

"No."

"Nothing can prepare you."

"I'm afraid I don't understand."

He looked at me out of his tired cleric's face. "You'll see
soon enough. Why don't you come over to the officers' tent
afterwards? I'll be there drinking my nightly coffee."

He nodded, glanced down once more at the man on the cot,
and then left, dropping the tent flap behind him.

I don't know how long I stood there before I could bring
myself to remove the cloth from the man's face. By now, enough
people had warned me of what I would see that I was both
curious and apprehensive. There is a myth about doctors not
being shocked by certain terrible wounds and injuries. Of
course we are but we must get past that shock—or, more

honestly, put it aside for a time—so that we can help the patient.

Close by, I could hear the feet of the guard in the damp grass, pacing back and forth in front of the tent. A barn owl and then a distant dog joined the sounds the guard made. Even more distant, there was cannon fire, the war never ceasing. The sky would flare silver like summer lightning. Men would suffer and die.

I reached down and took the cloth from the man's face.

"What do you suppose could have done that to his face, Father?" I asked the priest twenty minutes later.

We were having coffee. I smoked a cigar. The guttering candles smelled sweet and waxy.

"I'm not sure," the priest said.

"Have you ever seen anything like it?"

"Never."

I knew what I was about to say would surprise the priest. "He has no wounds."

"What?"

"I examined him thoroughly. There are no wounds anywhere on his body."

"But his face—"

I drew on my cigar, watched the expelled smoke move like a storm cloud across the flickering candle flame. "That's why I asked you if you'd ever seen anything like it."

"My God," the priest said, as if speaking to himself. "No wounds."

In the dream I was back on the battlefield on that frosty March morning two years ago when all my medical training had deserted me. Hundreds of corpses covered the ground where the battle had gone on for two days and two nights. You could see cannons mired in mud, the horses unable to pull them out.

You could see the grass littered with dishes and pans and kettles, and a blizzard of playing cards—all exploded across the battlefield when the Union army had made its final advance. But mostly there were the bodies—so young and so many—and many of them with mutilated faces. During this time of the war, both sides had begun to commit atrocities. The Yankees favored disfiguring Confederate dead and so they moved across the battlefield with Bowie knives that had been fashioned by sharpening with large files. They put deep gashes in the faces of the young men, tearing out eyes sometimes, even sawing off noses. In the woods that day we'd found a group of our soldiers who'd been mortally wounded but who'd lived for a time after the Yankees had left. Each corpse held in its hand some memento of the loved ones they'd left behind—a photograph, a letter, a lock of blonde hair. Their last sight had been of some homely yet profound endearment from the people they'd loved most.

This was the dream—nightmare, really—and I'd suffered it ever since I'd searched for survivors on that battlefield two years previous.

I was still in this dream-state when I heard the bugle announce the morning. I stumbled from my cot and went down to the creek to wash and shave. The day had begun.

Casualties were many that morning. I stood in the hospital tent watching as one stretcher after another bore man after man to the operating table. Most suffered from wounds inflicted by minie balls, fired from guns that could kill a man nearly a mile away.

By noon, my boots were again soaked with blood dripping from the table.

During the long day, I heard whispers of the man General Sullivan had quarantined from others. Apparently, the man had assumed the celebrity and fascination of a carnival sideshow. From the whispers, I gathered the guards were letting men in for quick looks at him, and then lookers came away shaken and frightened. These stories had the same impact as tales of spectres told around midnight campfires. Except this was daylight and the men—even the youngest of them— hardened soldiers. They should not have been so afraid but they were.

I couldn't get the sight of the man out of my mind, either. It haunted me no less than the battlefield I'd seen two years earlier.

During the afternoon, I went down to the creek and washed. I then went to the officers' tent and had stew and coffee. My arms were weary from surgery but I knew I would be working long into the night.

The General surprised me once again by joining me. "You've seen the soldier from Virginia?"

"Yes, sir."

"What do you make of him?"

I shrugged. "Shock, I suppose."

"But his face—"

"This is a war, General, and a damned bloody one. Not all men are like you. Not all men have iron constitutions."

He took my words as flattery, of course, as a military man would. I hadn't necessarily meant them that way. Military men could also be grossly vain and egotistical and insensitive beyond belief.

"Meaning what, exactly, Doctor?"

"Meaning that the soldier from Virginia may have become so horrified by what he saw that his face—" I shook my head. "You can see too much, too much death, General, and it can make you go insane."

"Are you saying he's insane?"

I shook my head. "I'm trying to find some explanation for his expression, General."

"You say there's no injury?"

"None that I can find."

"Yet he's not conscious."

"That's why I think of shock."

I was about to explain how shock works on the body—and how it could feasibly effect an expression like the one on the Virginia soldier's face—when a lieutenant rushed up to the General and breathlessly said, "You'd best come, sir. The tent where the soldier's quarantined—There's trouble!"

When we reached there, we found half the camp's soldiers surrounding the tent. Three and four deep, they were, and milling around idly. Not the sort of thing you wanted to see your men doing when there was a war going on. There were duties to perform and none of them were getting done.

A young soldier—thirteen or fourteen at most—stepped from the line and hurled his rifle at the General. The young soldier had tears running down his cheeks. "I don't want to fight any more, General."

The General slammed the butt of the rifle into the soldier's stomach. "Get hold of yourself, young man. You seem to forget we're fighting to save the Confederacy."

We went on down the line of glowering faces, to where two armed guards struggled to keep soldiers from looking into the tent. I was reminded again of a sideshow—some irresistible spectacle everybody wanted to see.

The soldiers knew enough to open an avenue for the General. He strode inside the tent. The priest sat on a stool next to the cot. He had removed the cloth from the Virginia soldier's face and was staring fixedly at it.

The General pushed the priest aside, took up the cloth used as a covering, and started to drop it across the soldier's face—then stopped abruptly. Even General Sullivan, in his rage, was moved by what he saw. He jerked back momentarily, his eyes unable to lift from the soldier's face. He handed the cloth to the priest. "You cover his face now, Father. And you keep it covered. I hereby forbid any man in this camp to look at this soldier's face ever again. Do you understand?"

Then he stormed from the tent.

The priest reluctantly obliged.

Then he angled his head up to me. "It won't be the same any more, Doctor."

"What won't?"

"The camp. Every man in here has now seen his face." He nodded back to the soldier on the cot. "They'll never be the same again. I promise you."

In the evening, I ate stew and biscuits, and sipped at a small glass of wine. I was, as usual, in the officers' tent when the priest came and found me.

For a time, he said nothing beyond his greeting. Simply watched me at my meal, and then stared out the open flap at the camp' preparing for evening, the fires in the center of the encampment, the weary men bedding down. Many of them, healed now, would be back in the battle within two days or less.

"I spent an hour with him this afternoon," the priest said.

"The quarantined man?"

"Yes." The priest nodded. "Do you know some of the men have visited him five or six times?"

The way the priest spoke, I sensed he was gloating over the fact that the men were disobeying the General's orders. "Why don't the guards stop them?"

"The guards are in visiting him, too."

"The man says nothing. How can it be a visit?"

"He says nothing with his tongue. He says a great deal with his face." He paused, eyed me levelly. "I need to tell you something. You're the only man in this camp who will believe me." He sounded frantic. I almost felt sorry for him.

"Tell me what?"

"The man—he's not what we think."

"No?"

"No; his face—" He shook his head. "It's God's face."

"I see."

The priest smiled. "I know how I must sound."

"You've seen a great deal of suffering, Father. It wears on a person."

"It's God's face. I had a dream last night. The man's face shows us God's displeasure with the war. That's why the men are so moved when they see the man." He sighed, seeing he was not convincing me. "You say yourself he hasn't been wounded."

"That's true."

"And that all his vital signs seem normal."

"True enough, Father."

"Yet he's in some kind of shock."

"That seems to be his problem, yes."

The priest shook his head. "No, his real problem is that he's become overwhelmed by the suffering he's seen in this war— what both sides have done to the other. All the pain. That's why there's so much sorrow on his face—and that's what the men are responding to. The grief on his face is the same grief they feel in their hearts. God's face."

"Once we get him to a real field hospital—"

And it was then we heard the rifle shots.

The periphery of the encampment was heavily protected, we'd never heard firing this close.

The priest and I ran outside.

General Sullivan stood next to a group of young men with weapons. Several yards ahead, near the edge of the camp, lay three bodies, shadowy in the light of the campfire. One of the fallen men moaned. All three men wore our own gray uniforms.

Sullivan glowered at me. "Deserters."

"But you shot them in the back," I said.

"Perhaps you didn't hear me, Doctor. The men were deserting. They'd packed their belongings and were heading out."

One of the young men who'd done the shooting said, "It was the man's face, sir."

Sullivan wheeled on him. "It was what?"

"The quarantined man, sir. His face. These men said it made them sad and they had to see families back in Missouri, and that they were just going to leave no matter what."

"Poppycock," Sullivan said. "They left because they were cowards."

I left to take care of the fallen man who was crying out for help.

In the middle of the night, I heard more guns being fired. I lay on my cot, knowing it wasn't Yankees being fired at. It was our own deserters.

I dressed and went over to the tent where the quarantined man lay. Two young farm boys in ill-fitting gray uniforms stood over him. They might have been mourners standing over a coffin. They said nothing. Just stared at the man.

In the dim lamplight, I knelt down next to him. His vitals still seemed good, his heartbeat especially. I stood up, next to the two boys, and looked down on him myself. There was nothing remarkable about his face. He could have been any of thousands of men serving on either side.

Except for the grief.

This time I felt the tug of it myself, heard in my mind the cries of the dying I'd been unable to save, saw the families and farms and homes destroyed as the war moved across the countryside, heard children crying out for dead parents, and parents sobbing over the bodies of their dead children. It was all there in his face, perfectly reflected, and I thought then of what the priest had said, that this was God's face, God's sorrow and displeasure with us.

The explosion came, then.

While the two soldiers next to me didn't seem to hear it at all, I rushed from the tent to the center of camp.

Several young soldiers stood near the ammunition cache. Someone had set fire to it. Ammunition was exploding everywhere, flares of red and yellow and gas-jet blue against the night. Men everywhere ducked for cover behind wagons and trees and boulders.

Into this scene, seemingly unafraid and looking like the lead actor in a stage production of King Lear I'd once seen, strode General Sullivan, still tugging on his heavy uniform jacket.

He went over to two soldiers who stood, seemingly unfazed, before the ammunition cache. Between explosions I could hear him shouting, "Did you set this fire?"

And they nodded.

Sullivan, as much in bafflement as anger, shook his head. He signaled for the guards to come and arrest these men.

As the soldiers were passing by me, I heard one of them say to a guard, "After I saw his face, I knew I had to do this. I had to stop the war."

Within an hour, the flames died and the explosions ceased. The night was almost ominously quiet. There were a few hours before dawn, so I tried to sleep some more.

I dreamed of Virginia, green Virginia in the spring, and the creek where I'd fished as a boy, and how the sun had felt on my back and arms and head. There was no surgical table in my dream, nor were my shoes soaked with blood.

Around dawn somebody began shaking me. It was Sullivan's personal lieutenant. "The priest has been shot. Come quickly, Doctor."

I didn't even dress fully, just pulled on my trousers over the legs of my long underwear.

A dozen soldiers stood outside the tent looking confused and defeated and sad. I went inside.

The priest lay in his tent. His cassock had been torn away. A bloody hole made a target-like circle on his stomach.

Above his cot stood General Sullivan, a pistol in his hand.

I knelt next to the cot and examined the priest. His vital signs were faint and growing fainter. He had at most a few minutes to live.

I looked up at the General. "What happened?"

The General nodded for the lieutenant to leave. The man saluted and then went out into the gray dawn.

"I had to shoot him," General Sullivan said.

I stood up. "You had to shoot a priest?"

"He was trying to stop me."

"From what?"

Then I noticed for the first time the knife scabbard on the General's belt. Blood streaked its sides. The hilt of the knife was sticky with blood. So were the General's hands. I thought of how Yankee troops had begun disfiguring the faces of our dead on the battlefield.

He said, "I have a war to fight, Doctor. The men—the way they were reacting to the man's face—" He paused and touched the bloody hilt of the knife. "I took care of him. And the priest came in while I was doing it and went insane. He started hitting me, trying to stop me and—" He looked down at the priest. "I didn't have any choice, Doctor. I hope you believe me."

A few minutes later, the priest died.

I started to leave the tent. General Sullivan put a hand on my shoulder. "I know you don't care very much for me, Doctor, but I hope you understand me at least a little. I can't win a war when men desert and blow up ammunition dumps and start questioning the worthiness of the war itself. I had to do what I did. I hope someday you'll understand."

I went out into the dawn. The air smelled of campfires and coffee. Now the men were busy scurrying around, preparing for war. The way they had been before the man had been brought here in the buckboard.

I went over to the tent where he was kept and asked the guard to let me inside. "The General said nobody's allowed inside, Doctor."

I shoved the boy aside and strode into the tent.

The cloth was still over his face, only now it was soaked with blood. I raised the cloth and looked at him. Even for a doctor, the sight was horrible. The General had ripped out his eyes and sawed off his nose. His cheeks carried deep gullies where the knife had been dug in deep.

He was dead. The shock of the defacement had killed him. Sickened, I looked away.

The flap was thrown back, then, and there stood General Sullivan. "We're going to bury him now, Doctor."

In minutes, the dead soldier was inside a pine box borne up a hill of long grass waving in a chill wind. The rains came, hard rains, before they'd turned even two shovelfuls of earth.

Then, from a distance over the hill, came the thunder of cannon and the cry of the dying.

The face that reminded us of what we were doing to each other was no more. It had been made ugly, robbed of its sorrowful beauty.

He was buried quickly and without benefit of clergy—the priest himself having been buried an hour earlier—and when the ceremony was finished, we returned to camp and war.

Gunslinger

HE REACHES Los Angeles three days early, a scrawny forty-eight-year-old man in a three-piece black Cheviot suit made of wool and far too hot for the desertlike climate here. He chews without pause on stick after stick of White's Yucatan gum. He carries, tucked in his trousers beneath his vest, a Navy Colt that belonged to his father, a farmer from Morgan County, Missouri.

As he steps down from the train, a Negro porter accidentally bumping into him and tipping his red cap in apology, he takes one more look at the newspaper he has been reading for the last one hundred miles of his journey, the prime headline of which details President Teddy Roosevelt's hunting trip to the Badlands, the secondary headline being concerned with the annexation by Los Angeles of San Pedro and Wilmington, thereby giving the city a harbor. But it is the third headline that holds his interest: DIRECTOR THOMAS INCE, NOW RECOVERED FROM HEART TROUBLE, STARTS NEW PICTURE THURSDAY WITH HIS FAMOUS WESTERN STAR REX SWANSON.

Today was Monday.

He finds a rooming house two blocks from a bar called The Waterhole, which is where most of the cowboys hang out. Because real ranches in the west have fallen on hard times, the cowboys had little choice but to drift to Los Angeles to become extras and stunt riders and trick shooters in the silent movie industry. Now there is a whole colony, a whole sub-culture of them out here, and they are much given to drink and even more given to violence. So he must be careful around them, very careful.

In the street below his room runs a trolley car, its tingling bell the friendliest sound in this arid city of 'dobe buildings for the poor and unimaginable mansions for the rich. It is said, at least back in Missouri, that at least once a day a Los Angeles police officer draws down on a man and kills him. He has no reason to doubt this as he falls asleep on the cot in the hot shabby room with its flowered vase lamp, the kerosene flame flickering into the dusk as his exhausted snoring begins.

In the morning he goes down the hall, waits till a Mexican woman comes out of the bathroom smelling sweetly of perfume, and then goes in and bathes and puts on the things he bought just before leaving Morgan County. A bank teller, he is not particularly familiar with real Western attire, but he knew it would be a mistake to buy his things new. That would mark him as a dude for certain. He had found a livery up in the northern edge of the county that had some old clothes in the back, which he bought for $1.50 total.

Now, looking at himself in the mirror, trying to be as objective as he can, he sees that he does not look so bad. Not so bad at all. The graying hair helps. Not shaving helps. And he's always been capable of a certain blue evil eye (as are most of the men in his family). Then there are the clothes. The dusty brown Stetson creased cowhand-style. The faded denim shirt. The Levi's with patches in knee and butt. The black Texas boots.

For the first time he loses some of his fear.

For the first time there is within him excitement.

In his room, before leaving, he writes a quick letter.

Dear Mother,

By the time you read this, you will know what I have
done. I apologize for the pain and humiliation my action
will cause you but I'm sure you will understand why I had
to do this.

If it were not for the man I will kill Thursday, you would
have had a husband all these years, and I a father.

I will write you one more letter before Thursday.

Your loving son,
Todd

The next two days . . .

In the Los Angeles of the movie cowboy extra, there are
certain key places to go for work. On Sunset Boulevard there is
a horse barn where you wait like farmhands to be picked for a
day's work; then there are a few studio backlots where you can
stand in the baking sun all day waiting for somebody already
hired to keel over and need to be replaced; and then there is
Universal's slave-galley arrangement where extras are literally
herded into a big cage to wait to be called. Five dollars a day
is the pay, which for some men is five times what they were
getting back in the blizzard country of Montana and Wyoming
and Utah.

It is into this world he slips now, making the rounds, trying
to get himself hired as an extra. If he does not get on Ince's set
Thursday, if he does not get that close, then he will be unable
to do what he has waited most of his life to do.

He is accepted. Or at least none of the other cowboys
question him. They talk in their rough boozy way of doing stunt
work—something called the "Running W" or the even more
frightening "Dead Man's Fall" are particularly popular top-
ics—and they gossip about the movie stars themselves. Which
sweet young virginal types can actually be had by just about
anybody who has taken a bath in the past month. Which so-

called he-men are actually prancing nancies afraid to even get close to a horse.

All this fascinates and frightens him. He wants to be back home in Morgan County, Missouri.

All that keeps him going is his memory of his father. The pennies on Father's eyes during the wake. The waxen look in the coffin. The smell of funeral flowers. His mother weeping, weeping.

The Navy Colt burns in his waistband. Burns . . .

Late on Wednesday, near the corral on the Miller Brothers 101 Ranch where Ince makes his two-reelers, a fat bald casting director in jodhpurs comes over and says, "You five men there. Can you be here at sunup?"

He has traveled fifteen hundred miles and forty-one years for this moment.

Dear Mother,

I never told you about where I saw him first, in the nickelodeon six years ago. He used a different name, of course, but I've seen so many photographs of him that even with his dyed hair and new mustache I knew it was him. I see now that his whole so-called "murder" was nothing more than a ruse to let him escape justice. He is not dead; he's alive out here . . .

He is very popular, of course, especially with the ladies, just as he was back there. He is also celebrated as a movie hero. But we know differently, don't we? If Father hadn't been riding back from the state capital that day on the train . . .

In the morning I go out to the Miller ranch where the picture is to be shot.

It will not be the only thing being shot . . .

Say hello to Aunt Eunice for me and think of me when you're making mince meat pie next Thanksgiving.

I think of your smile, Mother. I think of it all the time.

Your loving son,

Todd

All he can liken it to was his six-month stint in the army (six months only because of what the post doctor called his "nervous condition")—hundreds of extras milling around for a big scene in which a railroad car is to be held up and then robbers and good citizens alike are attacked by an entire tribe of savage Indians. It is in this way that the robber will become a hero—he will be forced to save the lives of the very passengers whom he was robbing.

The trolley car ran late. He did not sleep well. He urinates a lot. He paces a lot. He mooches two pre-rolls from a Texas cowhand who keeps talking about what a nancy the casting director in the jodhpurs is. The smoke, as always, makes him cough. But it helps calm him. The "nervous condition" being something he's always suffered from.

For two hours, waiting for the casting director to call him, he wanders the ranch, looks at the rope corral, the ranch house, the two hundred yards of train track meant to simulate miles of train track. There's even a replica of the engine from the Great Northern standing there. Everything is hot, dusty. He urinates a lot.

Around ten he sees Rex Swanson.

Rex is taller than he expected and more handsome. Dressed in a white Stetson, white western shirt with blue pearl buttons, white sheepskin vest and matching chaps, and enough rouge and lipstick to make him look womanly. Rex has just arrived, being dispatched from the back of a limousine long enough to house thirty people. He is instantly surrounded and in the tone of everybody about him there is a note of supplication.

Please Rex this.
Please Rex that.
Please Rex.
Rex *please*.

Just before lunch he sees his chance.

He has drifted over to a small stage where a painted back-drop depicts the interior of a railroad car.

It is here that Rex, in character, holds up the rich pas-sengers, a kerchief over his face, twin silver Peacemakers shining in his hands. He demands their money, gold, jewelry.

A camera rolls; an always-angry director shouts obscenities through a megaphone. Everybody, particularly the casting director, looks nervous.

His father knocking a baseball to him. His father bouncing him on his knee. His father driving the three of them—how good it felt to be the-three-of-them, mother son father—in the buggy to Sunday church. Then his father happening to be on the train that day/so waxen in the coffin/pennies on his eyes.

He moves now.

Past the director who is already shouting at him.

Past the actors who play the passengers.

Right up to Rex himself.

"You killed my father," he hears himself say, jerking the Navy Colt from his waistband. "Thirty-seven years ago in Morgan County, Missouri!"

Rex, frantic, shouts to somebody. "Lenny! My God, it's that lunatic who's been writing me letters all these years!"

"But I know who you really are. You're really Jesse!" he says, fear gone once again, pure excitement now.

Rex—now it's his turn to be the supplicant—says, "I'm an actor from New Jersey. I only play Jesse James in these pic-tures! I only *play* him!"

But he has come a long ways, fifteen hundred miles and forty-one years, for this moment.

He starts firing.

It takes him three bullets, but he gets it done, he does what Robert Ford only supposedly did. He kills Jesse James.

Then he turns to answer the fire of the cowboys who are now shooting at him.

He smiles. The way that special breed of men in the nickelodeons always do.

The gunslingers.

Guild and the Indian

Woman

THAT WAS THE autumn President Chester Alan Arthur fought hard for higher tariffs (or at least as hard as President Chester Alan Arthur ever fought for anything), and it was the autumn that Britain occupied Egypt. It was also the year that Leo Guild, a bounty hunter who sometimes described himself as a "free-lance lawman," pursued through the northeastern edge of the territory a man named Rogers. It was said that Rogers had killed a woman in the course of a bank robbery, though by all accounts the woman had been killed accidentally when Rogers tripped and the gun misfired. Guild did not care about the "accidentally" part. The owners of the bank were offering a $750 reward for Rogers. The spring and summer had not exactly made Guild a rich man, so finding Rogers became important. The search went two months and one week and ended in a town called Drayton, where there had been a recent outbreak of cholera, eighteen citizens dead, and three times as many sick. On a public notice listing the dead, Guild saw Rogers's name. But not being an especially trusting man, Guild went down the board sidewalk between the one- and two-story frame false fronts, alongside the jingle and clang and squeak of freight wagons and farm wagons and buggies, and found the local doctor's office.

Guild sat in Dr. McGivern's waiting room while, from behind the door, he heard McGivern giving instructions to a man
who coughed consumptively. Guild touched the knife scar on
the cleft of his chin and then rubbed his leg, still stiff from
a boyhood riding accident. The injury caused him to limp
slightly, especially now that gray November cold had set in.

He sat on a tufted leather couch across from a matching
chair and beneath two paintings of very idyllic Indians looking
noble in profile at breathtaking sunsets. The territory had not
been kind to Indians (and for that matter, Indians, except
perhaps for the Mesquakie, had not been kind to the territory),
so it was unlikely you'd find such specimens as these in the
paintings. On a table in front of the couch was a row of books
held upright by bookends molded into the shape of lions'
heads. Books by Longfellow, Hugo, Browning, and Tennyson
shared space with medical books entitled *The Ladies' Medical
Guide* by Dr. S. Pancoast, *Science of Life or Creative and Sexual
Science* by Professor O. S. Fowler, and *Robb's Family Physi-
cian*. In a corner of the waiting room a potbellied stove glowed
red with soft coal behind its grates.

The door opened and a stubby man with watery eyes and
filthy, shapeless clothes emerged. He needed a shave and a
bath. With the coast-to-coast railroad tracks and another cycle
of bank failures, the territory was home to many men like him.
Drifting. Dead in certain spiritual respects. Just drifting.
Guild knew he was cleaner and stronger and smarter, but he
was probably not very different from this man. So he was careful not to allow himself even the smallest feeling of superiority.

"You take this syrup for seven days and get all the rest you
can and you'll be fine," Dr. McGivern said, following his
patient into the waiting room. He was a tall, slender man in a
three-piece undertaker's suit. He had the prissy mouth and
pitiless eyes of a parson. He was pink bald and had a pair of
store-boughts that gave his mouth an eerie smile even though

he wasn't smiling at all. Guild, who tended to like people or not like people right off, did not like the doctor a whit.

The doctor put out his hand, and the coughing man put some coins in the doctor's palm.

"You sure it ain't the consumption, then?" the man said, obviously afraid.

"If it is, you'll know soon enough," the doctor said. His voice was as hard as his eyes. The patient had wanted something to be said softer. More reassuring. There was nothing soft about the doctor at all.

After the man left, the doctor pulled out a gold watch from his black vest pocket, consulted it importantly, and said, "I have a meeting at the bank in ten minutes." He pointed to his inner chamber. "Let's go in and have a look at you."

"I'm not here on medical business," Guild said. His dislike of the man was obvious in his voice. Maybe too obvious. Guild thought about the drifter who'd just left, thought about his fear. The doctor could have set his mind to rest. Hell, that should be a doctor's most important duty, anyway, even more than dispensing medicine. Setting minds to rest.

Now the doctor dropped all semblance of patience. "You don't look like a drummer, and I'm through buying cattle for my ranch. So just what would your business be?"

"I want to make sure a man died."

"What man?"

"Lyle Thomas Rogers. Cholera. Few weeks ago."

"You're a relative?"

"I was trying to locate him."

"Now there's a nice ambiguous sentence."

Guild looked back at the books on the table of the waiting room. The doctor was obviously an educated man, and spoke like one.

"Your business is what, exactly?" the doctor said.

"I'm a free-lance lawman."

"Meaning?"

Guild felt as if he were five years old and being challenged by a teacher. "Meaning, sometimes I track people."

This time the store-boughts really did smile. "My God, what vultures you people are. You're a bounty hunter." The doctor stuffed his watch back into his vest pocket and laughed. His laugh was hard, too. "You were tracking this Lyle Thomas Rogers, but death cheated you out of a bounty, is that it?"

"Then you buried him?"

"I did indeed." He spoke now with obstinate pleasure.

Guild fixed his Stetson back on. He wanted to go down the street to the restaurant and have sausage and eggs and fried potatoes, and then he wanted to go over to one of the saloons and have a single shot of bourbon, and then he wanted to leave town.

Guild was about to thank the doctor for his time when the door opened up and a small Mesquakie Indian woman came in. She was barely five feet. She was probably in her sixties, or maybe even her seventies. She was dressed in a shabby gingham dress and a shawl. She wore tawny scuffed leather moccasins and thick green socks. She had a small, fierce nose and disturbing, dark eyes. She had so many facial wrinkles, she reminded Guild of the monkeys in the St. Louis Zoo.

"Ko ta to," the doctor said, pronouncing her name with a precision that was a bit too educated to seem comfortable. "What are you doing here?"

Guild got the odd impression the doctor was afraid of the woman.

Then he knew why.

From inside her shawl she took a Colt Peacemaker, nine long silver inches of barrel, and proceeded to put two bullets in the doctor's face, and two more in his chest.

McGivern barely had time to scream before he slumped to the floor.

The small room, with its flowered wallpaper and comfortable hooked rugs, felt alien now. Gunsmoke lent the air tartness, and the gunshots, so many and so close, had deafened Guild momentarily.

He started to draw his own Navy Colt, but the Indian woman said, "It is not necessary. It was only McGivern I wanted to harm." She handed Guild the Colt and said, "You will walk with me to the sheriff's office?"

The sheriff was named Lynott. He was fifty something, as tall as Guild, white-haired. He wore an impressive silver star on the flap pocket of his gray wool shirt, and an identical star on the front of his brown Stetson. Apparently he wanted you to make no mistake about who was sheriff in Drayton.

He poured Guild's coffee into a tin cup and then handed it over across the desk and said, "You going to take your eyes down from my wall?"

"It's my business," Guild said, referring to the rows of wanted posters the sheriff had thumbtacked to a section of the green east wall. The sheriff's office was a busy place. A civilian Negro drug bucket and mop along and scrubbed the already clean floors while deputies in khaki pushed sad and angry prisoners into and out of the cell block, most likely back and forth to a nearby courthouse. Behind Guild in the big, clean offices sat a deputy with his feet up on the desk and a Winchester .22 repeating rifle in his lap. Another deputy worked laboriously over a typewriter using two fingers.

Lynott said, "I want you to think real careful."

"Hell."

"What?"

"She didn't say anything, Lynott. Nothing that meant anything. You've asked me four times."

"She just walked in and looked at him and shot him?"

"That's about it."

– 27 –

"But not a word more?"

"She asked me if I'd walk her over here."

"Now, why the hell would Ko ta to want to shoot the doctor?"

"Go ask her."

"She's sittin' back there, and she won't say a word. I sent in a priest, I sent in a minister, I sent in a female newspaper editor, and she won't say a word. Not a damn word."

"She got any kin?"

Lynott shrugged. "There's a small group of wickiups near up the boots. Mesquakies. Harmless, pretty much. Guess I'm gonna have to ride up there." Lynott looked very unhappy.

The deputy with the Winchester in his lap said, "They're still out there." From where he sat, he could see out the window.

Lynott said to Guild, "The whole town's upset. Take a look out the window."

Sighing—he wanted to leave; he'd been here nearly three hours now—Guild drug himself to his feet and looked out through the barred window and saw several small groups of citizens along the two-block expanse of board sidewalk. Some of the men wore homburgs. Some of the women wore sateen wrappers. It was getting to be a fancy place, Drayton was. Most likely the town would be like this—everybody whispering, speculating—until the old lady was sent to prison.

"He pretty popular?" Guild said, coming away from the window.

"Nope."

"Thought docs usually were."

"Cold type."

Guild thought about McGivern, recalling the way he'd treated the drifter. "Guess he was." Guild stayed on his feet, finished his coffee.

Lynott said, "I'd like you to stay around for at least the night. Inquest'll be tomorrow morning. All the goddamn rules and regs we got in this territory, I've got to be sure and do this right."

"I'm kind of flat. Hotel rooms cost money."

"Not when your cousin owns the hotel."

"Meaning the cousin would put me up free?"

"His name's Pete. Tell him you're my guest."

"I won't argue against a bed and clean sheets."

Lynott smiled. "Who said they'll be clean?"

The Parker House surprised him. Not only were the sheets clean, there were attractive young housemaids with courteous manners. Posters advertised a viola concerto by one Mrs. Robertson after supper. Being three weeks from a tub, Guild took advantage of the sheriff's largesse by taking a cigar and a magazine and then sitting in a hot, sudsy tin tub for half an hour. Such moments could sometimes be perilous because they gave him too much time to think, to remember. Stalking a man four years earlier, he'd made a terrible and unforgivable mistake. By accident he'd killed a six-year-old girl. A jury had reluctantly found him not guilty. Guild wished he could render the same verdict unto himself, but as his nightmares and vexations proved, he could not. Occasionally, though he was a Lutheran, he went to Catholic Confession, and sometimes that helped. Sometimes.

He ate a combination of breakfast and lunch and then went out into the streets. Guild always knew when there'd been a killing in a town. Despite the way Eastern papers liked to depict the territory, a terrible reverence was paid to murder here, and one could see that reverence—part anger, part fear (any death reminded you of your own), part excitement—on the faces of even the children.

As he made his way to a saloon down toward a spur in the tracks, he watched dead brown leaves scratch across the broad sidewalk, and he watched how people huddled into their heavy winter clothes. He wondered where he was going to spend the winter.

A railroad maintenance gang filled most of the saloon, farm kids mostly loud in their lack of book learning and zest for what they saw as "the city." They kept the player piano going and they kept the bartender going and they kept the single percentage going, several of the more eager ones dancing dances that made up in intensity what they lacked in grace. The percentage girl just looked sad. Guild felt uncomfortable watching her. Sometimes you wanted to help people. Usually there was nothing one could do. The sawdust on the floor needed sweeping out and replacing. It was tangy with hops and vomit. A drummer in a black double-breasted Chesterfield coat and a bowler sat at the end of the bar cadging slices of ham and cheese and slapping them with a curious precision to wide white slices of potato bread. Hard wind rattled the single glass window. Guild, standing at the bar, felt alone and old.

Guild had had two schooners and a shot of house bourbon, more than he'd intended for this time of day, when a voice said, "I understand you were the last person to see my father alive."

When he turned around, he saw one of those rarities—a son who looked an exact replica of his father. Usually the mother got in there somewhere—tilt of nose, color of eyes—but not in this case. The son was maybe thirty and already pink bald, and he carried himself with the same air of formality and peevishness his father had. He even wore the same kind of black three-piece suit. People grieved differently. Apparently for this man, anger was the worst part of the process because he looked as if he were barely able to keep himself under control.

Guild said, "I'm sorry about your father."

"I appreciate that." His tone said that Guild was wasting his time. "But I'm wondering what he said."

"He didn't have time to say anything."

"He just died?"

"He was shot with four bullets very quickly." Guild did not care for the son any more than he had the father.

"How about the Indian woman?"

Guild decided he was being unfair. Maybe these questions were the only way he could deal with his father's death. Guild said, "Why don't I buy you a drink and we'll leave the sheriff to figure it out."

"I'd really like an answer to my question."

"About the Indian woman?"

"Yes."

"She didn't say anything, except would I walk her to the sheriff's office."

"You're sure?"

"I'm sure."

Then the man did the damnedest thing of all. Obviously without meaning to, he sighed and smiled, as if a great and abiding relief had just washed through him. Then he said, "My name's Robert McGivern, Mr. Guild, and I'd be happy to have that drink with you."

Before suppertime, Guild decided to take a nap. He'd had many more drinks with Mr. Robert McGivern than he'd intended. McGivern was a strange one, no doubt about it, and one reason Guild had wanted to drink with him was to see when he'd break and show some simple human loss, but he hadn't. He'd talked about his importing business and he'd talked about his beautiful wife and his two beautiful children. He'd talked about the trips to New York City he took twice a year, and he'd talked about the territory someday becoming a state. But after finding out that neither his father nor the Indian woman had said anything to Guild, young McGivern seemed to lose interest in the subject. Guild wondered what McGivern had been so afraid might be revealed.

Spindly branches rasped against the window glass as the

November night deepened. Guild kept the kerosene lamp burning low. The light was a kind of company. He slept for an hour. He had a dream about the girl. She was dead now and in another realm. She stretched out her hand for Guild. He was afraid to take it. He wanted to take it but he was afraid. When the knocking came and woke him, he recalled the dream precisely, but he had no idea why he'd been afraid to take her hand. None at all.

He took his Navy Colt from the nightstand, stood up in his red long johns, and walked across the floor in the white winter socks he'd put on after bathing that morning. "Yes?" he said.

"Mr. Guild?"

"Yes."

"My name is Wa pa nu ke."

The name was Mesquakie. "What do you want?"

"I want to ask you some questions about my grandmother. She is the one who killed Dr. McGivern."

"Just a minute."

Guild went over and pulled on his serge trousers and then his boots. Then he went over to the bureau and poured water from a clay pitcher into a clay basin. He washed his face. He took a piece of Adams Pepsin Celery chewing gum, folded it in half, and then put it in his mouth. He picked up his Navy Colt again, and then went to let the Mesquakie into his room.

Wa pa nu ke turned out to be a chunky man in his twenties with a bad complexion and dark, guilty eyes. He wore loose denim clothes that accommodated his bulk. Guild could see that his ornate moccasins were decorated with deer's hair for the cold. He sensed a deep anger buried in the young Indian man, but he also sensed a curious temerity. It was not good to be red in a white man's world. Guild supposed it was that simple.

In five minutes Wa pa nu ke made his case very clear. He

believed that his grandmother was perfectly justified in killing the doctor.

"That's probably not a very smart thing to say out loud, at least not in Drayton," Guild said. He had turned the kerosene lamp up. Shadows gave the room a kind of beauty.

"If only my sister would tell me what happened."

"Your sister?"

"Yes, my mother died years ago of consumption. My grandmother raised us. She was like our mother. Something happened over the past five months, but my sister and grandmother would not tell me what. And I was gone during most of it."

"Gone where?"

"A railroad job. The Rock Island has Indian gangs."

"I see."

The Mesquakie glared at Guild. For the first time Guild sensed the man's pride. He was here to ask a favor—that was becoming obvious—but he did not much like asking white men for favors. Not much at all.

"The sheriff should talk to your sister," Guild said.

"In the first place, my sister will talk to no one. No one. In the second place, even if my sister told him something, he would not believe her. She's a Mesquakie."

Guild got out his pack of gum and offered Wa pa nu ke a stick. The Indian declined.

"I need your help, Mr. Guild."

"There really isn't much I can do."

"I have asked about you. You are a 'free-lance lawman,' I am told."

Guild smiled. "That's something of a misnomer, I'm afraid. Sometimes people don't like the phrase 'bounty hunter.' Sometimes I don't like it myself. So I say 'free-lance lawman.' It doesn't mean anything."

"I'd like you to come out in the morning and talk to my sister.

All she does is sob. She just keeps saying that she would like to help my grandmother, but that my grandmother would be angry if she tried."

"You really should talk to Lynott."

"I've told you about Lynott."

"It's not my concern."

"I have money saved from the Rock Island."

Guild sighed. The young Indian was as busted as Guild himself was. But he was willing to give it up. What choice did Guild have?

"Tell me where your wickiup is," Guild said.

"Do you want to be paid now?"

"How much you got saved, kid?"

"Eighty dollars."

"I'm going to try something first, and if that doesn't work, then I'll ride out to your wickiup. I'll want ten dollars."

"Only ten? I don't understand."

The Indian was as poor as Guild. "You don't need to."

For dinner Guild had steak, boiled potatoes, cabbage, sod corn, and beer. This was served in the cramped but nicely appointed dining room of the Parker House. He was smoking an Old Virginia cheroot and enjoying the way the light from the yellow brass Rochester lamps played off the red hair of a woman dining across the way. Then Lynott came in wearing his two badges (coat and Stetson) and came over and sat down at Guild's table. Lynott smelled of cigarettes and winter.

Guild said, "I was going to look you up tonight."

"I take it Wa pa nu ke came to see you."

"How'd you know that?"

"I listened to him talking to his grandmother in the jail house."

"You always eavesdrop that way?"

"Judge wants me to. Says what I hear can help him make a case he might not be able to otherwise."

Guild shrugged. "Makes sense."

"So you going to?"

"Going to what?"

"Help him?" Then Lynott nodded with his big badge-covered Stetson. "You got another cheroot?"

"You're the one gainfully employed, and I'm handing out the cheroots," Guild said wryly. "You'd think I was running for office." He set one down and Lynott took it.

Lynott lit up with a lucifer. He made rings exhaling. He said, "I don't really give a damn if you want to get involved, but it won't change the outcome any."

"You're not curious?"

"About why she shot him?"

"Yep."

"Nope."

"Why not?"

"It'd just keep things stirred up, an investigation." He had some more of his cheroot. It seemed to give him pleasure. He said, "Anyway, as I said, it won't change anything. You saw her shoot him in cold blood, right?"

"Right."

"And you're willing to testify to that, right?"

"Right."

"So who gives a damn why she shot him. She just shot him and that's it and that's all."

Guild said, "You know the son well? Robert?"

Lynott surprised him by flushing. Guild hadn't even been fishing particularly. But there it was. No reason at all for Lynott to get disturbed by the mention of the young McGivern, but he was very much disturbed.

"Some, I guess."

"We had some liquor today. He talks about himself a lot.

One of the things he talked about was how important he was, what with being majority stockholder in the bank and all. Is he important?"

"I guess." Lynott still looked uneasy. His cigar didn't seem to give him any pleasure. He kept touching his chest as if he had pains or gas. In the hazy yellow of the Rochester lamp he seemed old now, his hair very white, the skin of his face loose and sad.

"Is he important enough that if he asked you not to investigate, you'd oblige him?"

"That supposed to mean something?"

"It means what it means."

"No reason for us not to be friends, Guild." Lynott smiled. "You being a 'free-lance lawman' and all."

"I didn't like him."

"Robert?"

"Yep."

"Don't much myself."

"Then why help him out?"

"I'm fifty-eight. Drayton's supposed to retire me in two years with a pension. I've got a signed contract to that effect. Why jeopardize that—especially when lookin' into it won't change anything, anyway? She shot him and you're the witness and the subject's closed."

Guild wanted another bourbon, but he recalled the state of his finances. He said, "Since I provided the smoke, how about you providing the next drink?"

Lynott grinned. "Sure. My cousin Pete serves me free, anyway."

Guild said, "Maybe it's time I get myself a cousin named Pete."

In the morning Guild followed the directions Wa pa nu ke had given him. Guild rode at a trot along a stage road through the plains where everything in the light of the low gray sky looked forlorn, grass and sage and bushes all brown. Frost silvered much of the ragged undergrowth. Hermit thrushes and meadowlarks sounded cold. Guild huddled into his wool coat, collar upturned. His roan's nose was slick where snot had frozen. In five miles the terrain changed abruptly. The ground rose into scoria buttes of red volcanic rock. Below, where two magpies perched on an old buffalo skull, lay a valley. He brought the roan to the edge of it, and there on the red rock surface below (he had read newspaper speculation that the surface of the moon would look like this), he saw the wickiups. There were seven of them. They were shabby structures made of brush and saplings. You could smell prairie dog on the air. The Mesquakies, impoverished, ate prairie dogs frequently. Guild led the roan carefully down through the small, loose, treacherous rocks.

A malnourished mutt joined him soon, yipping at the roan. Then three Mesquakie elders appeared. They wore heavy clothing that was a mixture of white man and red man. They each wore huge necklaces made of animal bone and teeth. The eldest carried a long, carved stick that appeared to be a cane. He came up to Guild's roan and said, "You are the man Wa pa nu ke told us about?"

"Yes."

"Then would you leave, please? We are old here, and we do not trouble the white man. We do not want the white man to trouble us."

"I would like to see his sister."

"She has been ill for two months. She is ill even yet."

A few more Mesquakies drifted from their wickiups. They looked as old and malnourished as the dog who had snapped at the roan.

Guild dismounted. For effect he took his Winchester from its scabbard. Winchesters had a way of impressing people. Particularly old people with no defenses.

"I can only ask you not to speak with her," the elder of elders said.

Guild pointed with his rifle. The only wickiup from which nobody had come lay on the edge of the small settlement. "Is that hers?"

The elder of elders said nothing. There was just the sound of the wind making flapping sounds of the saplings on the wickiups. The roan whinnied and snorted. There was no other sound except high up, where the wind sounded like a flute in the red volcanic rock.

Guild went past the elders to the wickiup, where he suspected he'd find the girl.

She lay on a pile of buffalo skins with more skins over her. She was pale and sweaty. She trembled in the unmistakable way of cholera. Guild did not want to stay. Not with the virulence of cholera. But apparently she was getting better, because if it was going to kill her, it likely would have done so by now. The girl was perhaps in her late teens.

Guild said, "Your brother sent me."

She opened dark eyes that were vague with sickness. She was too toothy to be pretty, but she had very good cheeks and sensual lips.

"Will they hang my grandmother?" the Indian girl asked.

"I don't know. That could depend on what you tell me."

"My grandmother does not wish me to talk about it. She says it is a shameful thing. What I did and what the doctor did."

Obviously she wanted to tell him, had already hinted, in fact, at the course of her words. Guild said, "I heard her sob last night."

"My grandmother?"

"Yes. It was terrible, hearing her that way."

The Indian girl began to cry, and Guild knew his lie had worked.

"I should be the one who sobs—for what I have done, and for what the doctor did to my infant."

"Your infant?"

Wind threatened to tear the brush and sapling cover from the wickiup. The Indian girl used a corner of the place as her toilet, too weak to go elsewhere. Guild wanted to be outside the darkness and odor of this place.

"Yes," the Indian girl said. "Two months ago, when my brother was still away, Dr. McGivern helped me deliver my son."

"Where is your son now?"

"He is dead."

"How did he die?"

The Indian girl began weeping.

Four hours later, in Drayton, Guild rode his roan to the livery and then went straight to Lynott's office. The inquest was scheduled for three o'clock.

When he walked into Lynott's office, he saw a dozen well-dressed citizens, mostly men and mostly with cigars, sitting in straight-backed chairs around Lynott's desk. A fat man, whose gray, spaded beard lent him a satanic cast, sat in black judge's robes and brought down a gavel.

Guild slipped into a chair in the back row and listened as the proceedings began.

As Lynott had said, there wasn't much to debate. Guild was called and asked by the judge if the Indian woman known as Ko ta to had indeed murdered the doctor in cold blood. Guild said yes. He started to say something else, but then he saw Lynott and the judge exchange a certain kind of glance, and he knew that Robert McGivern could count not only the sheriff but also the judge among his good and true friends.

The inquest was over in twenty minutes.

"You think they'll hang her?"

"Don't know."

"I want your promise they won't. Otherwise I'll tell what I know."

"I've never been partial to threats, Guild."

Guild and Lynott stood outside the sheriff's office. As early dusk neared, the street traffic seemed in a hurry to go to its various destinations. He could smell snow on the wind. In these parts blizzards came fast.

Guild said, "You know what went on here. Why she killed him. Who's to say she wasn't right? At least she shouldn't die for what she did."

Lynott signed. "I guess I'd have to say you're right about that. That she shouldn't have to die."

"He was a goddamn killer, and the worst kind there is, and you know it."

Lynott dropped his eyes. "I know it. I won't dispute it." He sighed, touched a leather-gloved hand to the star on his coat. "I'll see that she doesn't hang, Guild. I promise you that. Now maybe it's time you ease on out of town."

Guild nodded to Robert McGivern, who was just emerging from the door with a very beautiful woman in a black dress, veil, and shawl. The rich always knew how to dress for funerals.

"I want one minute with him," Guild said.

"I don't want him hurt. You understand me?" Lynott's tone was angry.

Guild said, "He'll sign your pension checks, won't he?"

"I don't want him hurt."

"Just get him over here."

So Lynott went down the boardwalk and tipped his hat to Mrs. McGivern and whispered something to young Mr. McGivern and then nodded back to Guild.

Even from here, young Mr. McGivern looked scared. Lynott

had to give him a little push. Mrs. McGivern seemed very confused by it all. She scowled at Guild.

Guild took his arm enough to hurt him and then said, "I'm going to walk you over to that alley, and if you don't go with me, I'm going to shoot you right here. Do you understand me?" He spoke in a very soft voice.

"My God, my God." was all young McGivern in his three-piece could say.

Guild took him over to the alley and then went maybe twenty feet into it, behind the base of a wide stairway running up the back of a brick building, and Guild made it fast. He hit McGivern four times exactly in the ribs, and then three times exactly in the kidney. He felt a great deal of satisfaction when he saw blood bubble in McGivern's mouth.

"What the hell did you think that Indian girl was going to do to you, kid? She was just as ashamed of the fact that you got her pregnant as you were. Only you had to go to your old man and whine about it, so your old man wanted to make sure that nobody ever knew—certainly not the respectable folks around here—so he offered to deliver the baby for you, didn't he?"

McGivern, still sick and terrified from the beating he'd taken, could only nod.

"He smothered the baby, McGivern. Your old man, the doctor. He killed that baby in cold blood. That's why her grandmother shot him, and you know it. Ko ta to would have kept your secret, McGivern. She really would have."

He had been holding McGivern up by the coat collar. Now he let him drop to the hard mud floor of the alley. McGivern was crying and trying to vomit.

Guild left the alley then, and started toward the livery.

Lynott fell into step next to him. "I told you not to hurt him."

Guild stopped and eyed the other man without pity. "Somebody needed to hurt him, Lynott."

Guild went the rest of the way to the livery by himself.

Mainwaring's Gift

HE HAD BEEN nine hours riding to get here, Mainwaring had, and now that he was here, he wondered if he should have come at all.

Stover was little more than two blocks of false fronts, a railroad depot, telegraph lines, and a big livery stable to handle all the drovers who came through here in the hot months.

Not even on Christmas Eve was the plain ugliness of the little town softened any. The covered candles that should have given the main street a soft glow only succeeded in showing up the worn look of the buildings and the hard, hostile faces of the people. Stover was a boastfully religious town where no liquor was served except at one hotel and a man should know better than to trouble the ladies. There were long-standing tales of men who had done such and had found themselves hanging wrist-tied and black-tongued from a tree next to the winding river to the west.

A church half a block away was furious with yellow light and even more furious with a choir singing Christmas songs. Out here on the prairie the little white box split the night with its light and sound.

Mainwaring's horse sounded lonely coming down the street, its metal shoes striking the cold-hardened ground and smashing through occasional patches of silver ice. The horse smelled of manure and sweat. Mainwaring probably didn't smell much better.

Mainwaring was a cowhand when he could be and a farmhand when he needed to be. The hell of it, here in the Territory of 1892, was that with all the bank failures, tending sheep and pigs and crops paid a lot more than tending beeves. Too many big beef men had gone bust for bankers to climb right back on.

Most of this year, his thirty-sixth, Mainwaring had spent on sixty-three acres raising shell corn and soybeans and okra. He had been to town here twice, once in March when one of the other farmhands was afraid he'd come down with cholera (but hadn't), and the other to celebrate his birthday. For only the second time in his life, Mainwaring, who'd been raised to believe in the Bible himself, had found his way to a bottle of rye. Most of that night was fuzzy but he did remember making the acquaintance of a certain woman and that was what brought him here tonight. Though he'd written her several times since going back to the farm, he'd received no reply. He figured that maybe he'd use the night of Christmas Eve to sort of accidentally see her. Maybe in his drunkenness he had offended her in some way. He hoped not.

At the end of the first block he found the hotel where he'd met the town woman.

The lobby was nearly as bright as the church. Piney-smelling Christmas decorations hung from walls and doors, and a holiday tree that seemed to be near as high as the church spire stood in one corner, casting off the warm yellow-blue-red-green hues of Christmas candles.

The people in the lobby were about what you'd expect, relatively prosperous-looking folks in three-piece banker suits and silk and organdy dresses. Only prosperous people could afford such clothes.

Within thirty seconds of him entering the lobby, a glass of hot apple cider was thrust into Mainwaring's hand by the desk clerk, a stout man with a walrus mustache, a bald and shiny head, and a genuinely friendly manner.

As he handed Mainwaring the cider, he squinted one eye and said, "You look familiar."

Mainwaring, who was usually too embarrassed to talk when he was in gatherings like this—he was well aware that he was a yokel and that these townspeople were his betters—muttered something about spending his birthday here last spring.

"Why, that's wonderful!" said the desk clerk. "I hope you enjoyed the festivities!" he said, poking Mainwaring playfully in the ribs.

Then, abruptly, the clerk stopped himself, looked around at the other guests, who were just now starting to sing more Christmas favorites, and said, "My God, you're the one."

"The one?"

"This is an unbelievable coincidence."

"What is?"

"That you're here."

"It is?"

"Tonight of all nights."

"What is?"

Even though he knew the cider to be nonalcoholic, Mainwaring wondered if somebody might not have put something in this fellow's drink because he just wasn't making any sense.

The desk clerk looked even more furtive now, as if he were afraid somebody might overhear their conversation. He took Mainwaring by the sleeve and drew him closer to the counter. "You came to see her, didn't you?"

"Who?"

"Who? Why Jenny, of course."

Mainwaring felt like a ten-year-old. His face got hot with blood at the implication linking them together. "Well," he said.

The clerk whispered even more softly. "Believe me, friend, you don't know how glad she's going to be to see you."

"She tell you so?" Mainwaring felt his head and heart thrum

with excitement, though he tried to give the impression of being indifferent.

The clerk stared at him. "You don't know, do you?"

"Know what?"

"What happened to her."

"I guess maybe I don't."

The clerk leaned into him and nodded toward the group of people now starting to sing "Silent Night." "The people here have been awful to her."

"They have?"

"They point and they whisper and they condemn."

"Condemn?"

"Most all of them."

"But why?"

The clerk shook his head. "My God, man, can't you figure it out?"

He felt dense and more of a yokel than ever, Mainwaring did. But no matter how he berated himself for being stupid, he couldn't figure out what this man was talking about.

"Do you remember what you did that night?" the clerk asked.

Mainwaring tried a grin. "Got a little drunk."

"But that's all you remember?"

Mainwaring shrugged.

"She wasn't what she pretended to be," the clerk said.

"Huh?"

"Jenny. Don't you remember when she came into the saloon in the back there."

Mainwaring thought back and then flushed once more. "Oh. Yes. I sort of do now."

"She pretended to be a scarlet lady."

"Yes."

"But she wasn't."

"No, I didn't think so."

"She's the daughter of a man who was hanged here about a year ago for rustling some cattle. She went a little crazy after that and took to drink and wandered the streets here and gave everybody the impression that she'd become a lady of easy virtue. Sometimes she'd go out to where the mob hung him that night, and she'd stand under the tree and call out for her daddy as if he were gonna appear to her and answer." The clerk shook his head. "He never did, of course. Appear, I mean. But Jenny went right on cozying up to men and enjoying herself, so that she'd become a scandal in a town that was supposed to be without scandal. They threw her out several times but she kept coming back, kept cozying up to men in the saloon back there. But she never actually did anything with any of them."

"No?"

"No. Not until that night with you, that is."

"With me?"

"With you. She told me later on, after I'd given her some coffee and a cigarette, that she'd done it with you because there was an innocence about you that she liked and trusted. Something in your eyes, she kept saying." The clerk frowned. "Well, now that I've met you, I'd have to say you *are* a mite innocent— or something."

Somehow, Mainwaring didn't feel he was being complimented. "So what happened to her?"

"What happened? What do you think happened, fellow? She got with child. And that made her even more of a scandal. She'd walk everywhere, this unmarried woman with child, and say hello and nice day and how're you doing just as nice as pie, just as if nothing was wrong at all."

"They didn't like that, the townspeople?"

"Didn't like it? They tried threatening her out of town, and bribing her out of town, and even dragging her out of town. You know, they didn't feel it was fitting for a woman like her to show herself to our children."

"They didn't, huh?"

"Nope. But it didn't do any good. She was just as obstinate as ever. She might be gone for a day or two, but she always showed up again. Always. Then the accident happened and there wasn't much they could do, and still call themselves Christians and all."

"Accident?"

"Out near the tree where her daddy was hung."

"What happened?"

"Stagecoach. Running a couple hours late as usual and top speed. She'd been under the tree and wailing and carrying on the way she usually did, and she didn't hear the stage in the road and it ran her down."

"My Lord."

The clerk paused, his jowly face fallen into a look of despair. "She almost lost the baby. Would have if I hadn't took her in, put her in a guest room on the third floor. That's where she's been ever since."

Mainwaring raised his slate-blue eyes to the sweeping staircase before him.

"She's gonna have the baby any time now."

"She got a doctor?" Mainwaring asked.

The clerk glowered. "Nope. Only doc in town's afraid to help her because the good Christian people hereabouts won't like it. Oh, that isn't what he says, of course—he's got some other cock and bull explanation—but that's what it comes down to."

Mainwaring said, gently, "So what're you gonna do?"

The desk clerk popped his Ingram from the watch pocket of his vest and said, "Any time now, a granny woman from a farm ten miles north of here is comin' by. She's going to help her."

Mainwaring said, "You're trying to tell me this baby is mine, aren't you?"

The desk clerk laughed without humor. "Well, it took you a

while to figure out what was going on here, but maybe it was worth the wait." He nodded to the stairs. "Come on."

The room was in the rear, next to a fire exit.

The desk clerk stopped him outside the door. "I'm going in and talk to her a minute. Then I'll come and get you, all right?"

Mainwaring nodded.

While the clerk was gone, Mainwaring went over and looked out the back window. The night was black and starry. A quarter moon cast drab silver light on the small huddled town. Only the singing from the lobby below and the church nearby reminded Mainwaring of what night this was. He was still trying to make sense of this. He had come into town to see Jenny—all innocent enough—and now he was being told he was a father.

"She's ready for you," the clerk said when he came back. He closed the door behind him. "She's real sick, though. I wish that granny woman would get here."

Mainwaring went inside. He saw immediately what the desk clerk was talking about. The frail, blanched woman who lay belly-swollen and sweating in the middle of a jumble of covers was not the pretty fleshy girl of the spring. She had the look of all dying animals about her. Mainwaring felt scared and sick, the way he'd gotten just recently when he'd seen a foal dying in the barn hay a month ago. Animals, especially young and vulnerable animals, were Mainwaring's way of beating the loneliness of hardscrabble prairie life.

She lay on her back with her hands folded on her belly. Sweat had made her blond hair dark and her gray skin sleek.

He walked up to her and put his hand out and touched her folded hands.

"Hello," he said.

She opened her eyes then and he saw immediately how far gone she was.

She smiled, "I told him you'd come. Somehow."

"I came all right."

"Oscar said he told you about me and the baby."

"Oscar?"

"The desk clerk, Oscar Stern. You believe him?"

"That I'm the father?"

She nodded.

"Yes, ma'am, I do." His hat in his hand, gripping it now, he said "I hope I didn't—force you into anything that night."

"You didn't." She sounded as if even speaking were diffi-cult. "I got your letters."

"You did?"

"Yes."

"How come you didn't write? I sat there in my cabin at night and thought you didn't want nothing more to do with me."

She closed her eyes. "I guess I was afraid you wouldn't believe me. I figured you'd think that maybe some other man . . ."

She convulsed then, her fragile body threatening to snap in two. She moaned and he saw her eyes begin to dilate.

He turned and opened the door. "That granny lady here yet?" he asked Oscar Stern.

Just as Oscar was about to speak, a short woman in some kind of cape came up the stairs. She had a pipe in one corner of her mouth, a furious glare in her brown eyes, and a curse coming from her lips.

Suddenly, Mainwaring saw what she was angry about.

Right behind her came a tall, severe man in a cleric's collar and three hefty women in their holiday finery.

The granny woman pushed past Mainwaring and the desk clerk and went inside.

The minister spoke first. "Oscar, even though you're of another faith, this town has striven to abide our differences. But we've warned you all along what would happen if you permitted this woman to have her child within these city limits."

Oscar Stern said, "Even though I'm not a Christian, Pastor, I'm trying hard to act like one. Somebody's got to care for that girl."

"Not in this town they don't," said one of the ladies.

"We have a wagon downstairs," the minister said. "We plan to take her out to the Kruse farm where a midwife there will take care of her. We just don't want a . . ."

"We don't want an unmarried woman having her child in our town," said another of the women. "What kind of example do you think that sets?"

The minister was getting himself ready for another round of rhetoric, patting his silver hair and swelling his chest, when Mainwaring stepped forward.

"Anybody tries to move that woman," he said, "I'll get my rifle and kill him on the spot."

"My Lord," said the third woman. "Who is this man?"

"I happen," Mainwaring said, "to be the father."

Grave looks of displeasure crossed the faces of the four visitors. The minister looked as if he wanted to spit something awful-tasting from his mouth. He looked Mainwaring up and down and said, "I must say, you're just about the sort of man I would have expected to be the father."

"You get out of here now," Mainwaring told them. "Oscar Stern owns the hotel and it's his rules we abide by here."

One of the women started to say something.

Glaring, Mainwaring pointed his finger at her as if it were a weapon. The woman looked outraged and then she looked frightened.

"After tonight, Oscar," the minister said, "you may as well put this place up for sale. You won't be living in Stover much longer. I can promise you that."

The religious entourage left.

The granny woman, who had obviously been listening, stuck her head out the door and said, "One of you lazybones get in here. I need some help."

Birthing was scissors and thread and cloverine salve; birthing was sulfur and wine of cordia; birthing was cutting the cord and tying it off and dressing the baby; birthing was taking all the afterbirth, including the umbilical cord and placenta, and burying it out in the alley. After all this, the granny woman greased the infant's naval cord with castor oil and then added some powder to the oil.

During all this, Mainwaring sat in the room, terrified and joyous simultaneously, jumping up whenever the granny woman summoned him, carrying hot water and clean rags, ointment and liniment and salve.

When it was all over, when the infant was revealed to be a girl and Jenny herself was collapsed into an exhausted sleep, the granny woman left the child with Oscar and took Mainwaring out into the hall.

"You can see what's going on in there."

"Ma'am?"

"Jenny. She's dying."

Mainwaring felt colder than any winter night had ever made him feel. There was the unaccustomed sting of hot tears in his eyes. He said, "I love her."

"Right now, it's that little girl you've got to worry about."

"But—"

The granny woman said, "I know you love Jenny, son. But now, that don't matter. It's that child that matters."

Mainwaring went back inside the room. The granny woman gave him the infant and then left the room.

For half an hour Mainwaring sat next to the bed with dying Jenny. Occasionally she'd mutter something deep in the down-fathoms of her sleep, something that had the word daddy or father in it.

When the baby squalled, Mainwaring shushed and rocked it, thinking of all the tiny animals he had befriended over the years. This was the tiniest and most special animal of them all. His own daughter.

Finally, Jenny opened her eyes. Her mouth was parched and she could barely speak, but she spoke anyway. She smiled and looked up and touched their little girl there in Mainwaring's arms and said, "My daddy said she's beautiful."

Mainwaring said nothing.

"I saw my daddy just now. He's waiting for me."

Mainwaring felt the tears again and held the baby tighter.

"I'm sorry for how all this happened," Jenny said. "I should've written you back."

Mainwaring just shook his head.

"I want her to love you as much as I love my daddy," she said.

"I'm gonna give her every reason to love me," Mainwaring said. "I'm gonna be the best daddy she could ask for."

Jenny put her long, slender hand to Mainwaring's cheek. "You're not the smartest or the prettiest man I ever saw, Mainwaring, but I honestly do believe you're the best. And that's why I'm so glad I'm leaving her in your care."

He wasn't sure when she died—whether it was when she sighed and her entire body trembled; or when her face turned away from her little girl, toward the wall; or when her hand stretched out briefly in the air as if she were taking an unseen hand in her own—but when he leaned down to kiss her forehead and felt the stone coldness there, he knew.

He sat with his child in his arms, not even noticing how she cried now, just gently rocking her and looking at the dead woman, feeling occasionally the tears in his eyes and the hard unbidden lump in his throat.

After a time, Oscar Stern and the granny woman came back in. The granny woman saw to Jenny and the infant, and Oscar saw to Mainwaring.

"Where you going tonight, son?"

Mainwaring shook his head. "I'm not going to stay here. Probably start back for the farm."

"You think you can handle that infant?"

"The owner's got a wife and a young daughter. They'll help."

Oscar frowned. "Don't blame you for wanting to get out of this town. I'll be leaving it myself soon enough."

Mainwaring put out his hand. "I want to thank you."

"I should be thanking you, Mainwaring. You brought Jenny and me together, and she was one of the few decent people I've known in this place."

Mainwaring went back inside the room. Alone there, the door closed, he knelt beside the dead woman and held her hand for a long and silent time. There were no tears now, nor any unbidden lump in his throat, just his wonderment at her goodness and her grace, and his wish that he'd had time to know her well and love her as all his life he had longed to love a woman.

He stood up, went out and said good-bye to Oscar and the granny woman, and then he set off with the child.

Just as he was leaving town, he heard the church bell celebrate another birth on this night nearly two thousand years ago, and he wondered if people so soured by righteousness and so empty of compassion would love even Jesus if he were to come back.

He rode on, Mainwaring did, hard into the dark night and on Christmas morning crested a hill from which he could see the farm below. He could see smoke from its chimney and hear children singing carols. Farmers from all over the valley had gathered in this house.

Just before he took the horse down the rocky hill, he looked at his swaddled baby and smiled. During the night he had realized that he did, after all, have a woman to love.

His daughter.

Blood Truth

K ENDRICKS PUT the toe of a pointed boot to Helms's ribs and nudged hard. "Wake up. We're off-schedule already," he said. All the time he talked, Kendricks kept his Remington aimed straight at the kid's chest. Walter Helms had killed a man in an argument over a poker game, and he wasn't the sort you took chances with.

They were up near the Canadian border, in Toole County, east of Sunburst. This was a chill spring morning, as you could tell by the silver glaze of ice over the stream below and the frost on the bunch grass and sagebrush. The sky was a porcelain blue and the sun promised to warm the land later on.

Kendricks had trailed Helms to a rooming house on the edge of a prairie town in Alberta. He'd caught him in bed with a nice-looking redhead who probably wasn't old enough to be legal. Right off, Kendrick had seen the kid's pride, how embarrassed he was to be apprehended in front of a woman. But Walter Helms had said only one thing as Kendricks brought him down the back stairs, and that he said softly: "My turn'll come, bounty hunter. You wait and see." There hadn't even been any anger in the threat. He seemed to be just stating a fact.

Walter Helms sat up in his blankets and tried to shake off sleep. His blond hair was matted against his skull and his chin was stubbly with a light beard. He needed a shave and he needed a bath, but Kendricks figured the authorities could worry about that. The good people of Chinook planned to try the twenty-one-year-old and then quickly give him a proper hanging.

"I didn't get much sleep," Helms said, looking around the small, crude campsite. The fire had burned out and Kendricks had pitched dirt over it. Everything had been packed up on their horses. Kendricks hadn't even left the tin coffeepot out. "I kept having nightmares."

"So I heard," Kendricks said. "You kept me awake, too." But that wasn't all that had kept Kendricks awake. He'd kept thinking about what the kid had asked him yesterday. Kendricks had said no right away, but now he wondered if he shouldn't say yes.

Helms stared up at him with his strange blue eyes. The kid's gaze always looked innocent and slightly hurt. That's what fooled people. His gentleness. "You'd have nightmares, too, if you knew there was a rope waiting for you." The kid was always a gentleman; almost unnervingly so.

Kendricks's tone softened some. "I guess I would, kid. I guess I would." He nodded to the horses. "We'd better get going. Like I said, we're running behind schedule."

During the morning they worked their way across a broad plain that eventually gave way to scattered foothills. They were near Willow Creek now, heading south.

Kendricks sat a dun and rode slightly ahead of the kid, whom he'd handcuffed to his saddle horn. The kid was a talker and Kendricks hated talkers.

"You like your job, Mr. Kendricks?" Helms asked around noon. That was one of the kid's many eerie habits. Here he was, a cold-blooded killer, but he always sounded as proper and respectful as a schoolboy. It seemed to be one of the reasons that young females seemed to find him so dashing and fascinating. In a land of crude, even vulgar men, the kid had real style.

"It's all right, I guess."

"I'll bet it's hard work. Being a bounty hunter, I mean."

Kendricks looked back at him and shook his head. "Not near as hard as being a killer."

For half the afternoon they skirted low foothills. Helms's roan picked up a rock, and so they had to stop while Kendricks tried to fix the shoe. In the war one of his jobs had been apprentice to a blacksmith. He had some luck and the horse was soon walking smartly again.

In another hour the sky changed abruptly. Black clouds replaced the blue sky. You could smell rain coming.

"You remember what I asked you yesterday, Mr. Kendricks?"

"I remember."

"Well, we're not more than a half mile from it. Right over that ridge and down along a creek bend. And there it sits."

"I'm sorry, kid. I can't do it."

Helms brought his horse up next to Kendricks. His blue eyes showed innocence again. "You know what they're going to do to me, Mr. Kendricks. I only want to see her for an hour or so."

"Kid, I just don't think it's a good idea. And that's all I've got to say about it."

But the pain was back in the kid's gaze, and for some reason it struck Kendricks as genuine.

"Wouldn't you want to see your mother once before you died?" the kid said.

The rain started. It was hard, cold, numbing rain, and the horses hated it as much as their riders. This kind of weather always brought on Kendricks's arthritis. At forty-one, the former Helena lawman often got crippled fingers and painful knees from weather like this. And sleeping on cool ground wasn't going to make him feel any better, either.

They rode on. Kendricks thought things over. A farmhouse

sounded good. Most likely, she'd feed them well and bed them down pleasantly, and in the morning they could set off fresh and dry and make the last leg of their journey in one long day's ride.

Kendricks fell back in the pounding rain and shouted above the din, "You sure your ma's the only one there?"

"I'm sure."

"Then let's head there."

Even in the dusk, even through the slanting silver rain, Kendricks could see the kid's grin. He looked like a twelve-year-old who just won a prize at the county fair.

The soddy sat in a small bowl of sandy earth, ringed on three sides by junipers. This was a Kansas-style soddy which meant that the sod blocks probably weighed as much as fifty pounds each, with wooden frames carefully set in place for windows.

Now, just after dark, the only light was a kerosene lamp flickering faintly against the glass.

They took their horses to a rope corral around back and Kendricks fed them hay. Helms watched this, his hands still cuffed.

Kendricks went up to the door first and knocked. Apparently the rainfall had drowned out all sound of them arriving. After a time the door opened and a short, slender woman, just as good-looking as her son, stood warily looking out at him. The kerosene lamp back-lighted her head and gave her graying hair, tied up into a knot in the back, the sheen of gold.

"Hello, Mom," Helms said, stepping into the lamp-glow.

No mistaking the sound the woman made. A sob of pure joy. Nobody would greet heaven with any happier voice.

"Come in, come in," she said after hugging him and kissing him several times. She seemed not to notice Kendricks.

Kendricks followed them inside.

In a poor soddy like this you didn't expect to find much in the way of furnishings. But you could tell that the woman had tried to improve her hardscrabble life by adding a worn carpet to the floor and strips of gingham to the rough walls. Patchwork quilts decorated two straw-filled mattresses. A wooden dry-goods box had been covered with a small festive scrap of red cloth and now served as a table.

Only when she got her son inside, into the light, did she see the handcuffs. Then she glared at Kendricks, her eyes filled with accusation. "No need to tell me what you are, mister," she said.

"He's not so bad, Ma," Helms said gently. "He's just trying to make a living the same as we all are." Again, Helms sounded not like a snarling killer but more like an educated and most genteel young man. "I'd appreciate it if you'd fix us some dinner."

But the woman still glared at Kendricks. "I'll fix you some food, Walter, but I'll be darned if I fix him any."

The woman, whose name, he learned, was Grace, heated up some prairie chicken in the three-legged "baker" that stood over burning coals. She dished potatoes and biscuits onto her son's plate.

As she did this, Walter lay on the bed, staring at the ceiling. Kendricks sat in a rocking chair. Every once in a while the chair would squeak when he'd lean forward, but most of the time there was just the sound of the rain hammering away at the soddy's roof. The fire and the smell of the food made Kendricks feel comfortable and lucky. His stomach rumbled and a kind of sickness came over him when he saw how full Walter's plate was.

Grace Helms set the plate on the bed. Walter sat up. He still had the cuffs on, of course. His mother had to cut his meat for him.

About halfway through his meal Helms looked up at his mother, who was now back at the stove, and said, "Now, Ma. This isn't like you. Treating guests this way."

"He's no guest, Walter. He's a bounty hunter. The lowest form of life there is."

"Then do it for me," Walter Helms said. "For me, dish him a plate of good prairie chicken and biscuits and potatoes the way you did for me."

She looked over at him from the baker where she was stirring the broth. "You really want me to?" She looked pretty then, and younger, not so prairie-hard as she had in the doorway.

"Yes, Ma, I really want you to."

So Kendricks got his supper, after all, including a cup of very bitter coffee.

Around nine o'clock the rain became sleet. It sounded as if pellets were being fired against the roof.

Grace Helms had set a kerosene lamp on the floor next to her son's bed. He immediately picked up a month-old issue of the Great Falls *Tribune* and started reading it.

To Kendricks she said, "I want you to know something, Mister. That's an educated boy there. He got through fourth grade and he knows how to read Sir Walter Scott with no help from his teacher."

Helms put the newspaper down and looked over at Kendricks. He smiled. "I don't think you've convinced our friend here that I'm a model citizen, Ma."

"Well," she said, "what does he know anyway?"

Helms went back to reading. Grace sat across from him in a matching rocking chair. She darned socks with amazing efficiency.

For a time Kendricks sat with his head back and his eyes closed. His .44 sat in his lap. His rough hand was never more than an inch away from the trigger. He dozed and he listened to the sleet. He still felt snug and lucky about being in here tonight. He just wished he could keep his eyes open. Dozing off in this situation could be dangerous. . . .

The next time he sat up straight, he heard Walter snoring in his bed. His mother was standing over him, looking down at him. Kendricks couldn't recall ever seeing a more perfect portrait of grief. Within a month her son would be hanged.

Seeing that Kendricks was awake, she turned around and came back to her rocking chair.

"He used to sit there," she said. She spoke gently now. Her fingers flicked over the darning. "In the chair where you are."

"Walter, you mean?"

She shook her head. "No; his father."

"Oh."

"Died when Walter was eleven. Consumption."

"I'm sorry."

"Walter and I, we both miss him." She glanced over at her sleeping son again. The newspaper had fallen across his chest. She smiled at Walter and then looked back at Kendricks. "I'm sorry I was so harsh when you came in."

"I understand, ma'am. This isn't an easy thing."

"He's a good boy."

"I'm not judging him, ma'am."

"But you're taking him in."

"It's how I earn my living. It's nothing personal."

She seemed to study his face. He felt sleepy. He probably looked sleepy, too. "Would you like a little more chicken?"

"No thanks, ma'am."

"Then some more coffee, maybe."

He rubbed at his face, yawning. "Coffee sounds real good. I'd appreciate it."

She filled his tin cup and brought it back to him. He heard this rather than saw it. His eyes had closed again and he'd tilted his head against the back of the chair.

When the coffee came, he sat up straight and kept blinking his eyes. He seemed to be having a little trouble focusing.

Thank God for the coffee.

Grace Helms sat across from him again, doing her darning, staring at him. "Did you ever think he may not have done it?"

"As I said, ma'am, I don't judge him. That's up to the jury and the court."

"He wrote me a letter. He said it was a fair fight. He said that the man had accused Walter of cheating and drew his gun on Walter. Walter didn't have any choice but to draw his gun and defend himself."

Kendricks sighed. Maybe knowing the real facts would help her in some way. "From what I'm told, Walter was dealing a marked deck. The man picked up all his chips and tried to leave the game. Walter shot him in the back. The man was a farmer. He was unarmed." He spoke as softly as he could.

She didn't say anything now. She just sat there in the lamp-glow, the wind whining, the sleet raking the roof, and looked at Kendricks as if he'd just spoken in a language incomprehensible to her.

Finally, in barely a whisper, she said, "Is that the truth?"

"It's the truth as far as I know it, ma'am."

And then he yawned again. He liked sitting here across from her. Despite her fear and bitterness there was a soft quality he liked about her. He could imagine holding her in his arms; not even sex, not at first anyway, just holding her.

"Do you have a family, Mr. Kendricks?"

He took note of the "mister."

He shook his head. "Back when I was a town marshal in Helena, I had a wife. She was shot one day during a bank robbery. Completely innocent. She'd just gone in to make a deposit."

The woman sighed. "That's terrible, Mr. Kendricks. I'm sorry."

"So I went after the men who did it. It took me eight months and three states, but by God I found them and I turned them over for trial."

She started staring at him hard again, as if she were trying to decipher something in his expression. "And you've been chasing bad men ever since?"

"Ever since."

She nodded to the bed. "You've got my boy confused with the kind of men who killed your wife, Mr. Kendricks. But he's not like that at all. Not at all."

He felt sorry for her. He'd seen this in the parents of so many killers, how you told them the truth—that Walter Helms's victim had been shot in the back—but somehow they forgot right away and went back to seeing their boy as somebody the law was picking on.

He yawned again, and that was when he knew. His head started spinning and the hand he put to the armrest of the rocking chair trembled. "The coffee," he said. "You put something in the coffee."

"He's a good boy," Grace Helms said.

He tried to push himself up from the chair but he didn't have the strength. He just kept yawning; and his head kept spinning.

"The coffee," he said again, feeling drool run down his mouth. Whatever she'd put in there was enough to knock him out entirely.

By the time he'd sunk full into the chair again, his breath was coming loud and ragged. Everything before his eyes was being swallowed up in darkness.

Just before he opened his eyes, Kendricks made note of two things. One, he had to pee pretty bad. Two, he had a headache that was like getting your skull sawed in half.

He opened his eyes.

In front of the door, Walter Helms was tugging on his sheep-lined coat and strapping on the .44 and holster that had belonged to Kendricks.

Seeing that the bounty hunter was awake now, Helms said, "I was hoping for this, Kendricks." The young man's tone was different now. Gone was the almost toadying politeness. Cold rage filled his voice.

"You promised, Walter," his mother said, coming over to him. "You just git now and git fast. You can be fifty miles in any direction by the time he gets a horse."

But whatever was troubling Walter Helms was troubling him deep.

He lunged across the room and put the .44 into Kendricks's face. "You could've waited till I came downstairs and got me when I was alone, Kendricks. You didn't have to humiliate me in front of that girl."

So it was just as Kendricks had suspected. Helms had been angry over being taken while the girl was still with him. Some men were like that. To Kendricks it made no sense.

"Get up," Helms said.

"Walter," his mother said. She stood next to him, pawing at his sleeve like a frightened animal. "You just git gone now. You hear me?"

"He's going out the door with me," Walter Helms said.

Kendricks was still trying to come out of the sleep the coffee had put him into. His head ached and buzzed and he was still having trouble focusing his eyes.

"I said come on!" Walter Helms said. He put the cold barrel of the .44 hard against Kendricks's forehead.

Kendricks stood up.

Because of the coffee all this had a certain dreamy quality to it. His knees felt wobbly. He felt as if he were about to pitch forward.

"No!" Grace Helms said.

But Walter paid her no attention. He waved Kendricks to the door and outside.

As Kendricks reached the Helms woman he composed himself enough to say, "Still think he's a good boy, Mrs. Helms?"

"None of your back talk, bounty hunter," Walter Helms said, and gave Kendricks a rough push into the night.

The rain and sleet were coming down so hard Kendricks's flesh felt as if it were being struck by very sharp and very tiny pins.

He could see almost nothing as he staggered through fog and sleet, starting to slip on the soggy ground that was becoming icy.

Somewhere behind him Walter Helms's voice barked for Kendricks to stop. But why give the little son of a bitch the satisfaction, Kendricks thought. He's going to back-shoot me just the way he back-shot that farmer. So I may as well keep on walking.

Which is just what he did.

Knowing he was about to die, his thoughts formed something like a prayer. He sure could have been a better man than he'd been.

Knowing he was about to die, he conjured a picture of his young, pretty wife. He hoped that the afterlife wasn't just something ministers liked to talk about—he hoped he'd be seeing her soon.

And knowing he was about to die, he felt fear. It was shameful, this apprehension. It loosened his bowels and made his throat so tight he couldn't even swallow saliva. And it put tears in the corners of his eyes, too.

"I said for you to stop walking!" Walter Helms screamed somewhere back there in the darkness.

Soon enough, the shot would come.

Sleet cut his face like razors. Rain soaked his clothes and made them sodden. Ice gave his gait a comic aspect.

But he kept right on walking away from Helms.

There was but one shot, and the angry noise it made was mostly absorbed by the sleet and rain.

He expected to feel the bullet tear through his back and angle through his chest, ripping through his heart and lungs. A .44 could inflict a considerable amount of pain while it was killing you.

But the cry that slashed through the wind was not Kendricks's cry. It belonged instead to Walter Helms.

By the time Kendricks turned around to see what had happened, the kid had already fallen forward on his face. Several feet behind him, silhouetted in the yellow glow of the doorway, stood his mother. A rifle dangled from the fingers of her right hand.

Through the sleet and wind she called, "Will you help me get him inside, Mr. Kendricks?"

The vigil lasted till near dawn. Walter Helms was set in his bed and covered with two extra quilted blankets and given a seemingly unending supply of homeopathic medicines, including some of the herbs Grace had put in Kendricks's coffee.

But if any of it was doing any good the results weren't yet apparent, for Walter Helms looked as if he'd been laid out by a mortician. He grew more and more pale as the kerosene lamp flickered short on fuel.

Three times the widow got up and went to the door and stood in the blast of sleet and whining wind. And three times Kendricks could hear her sobbing quietly to herself before coming back to Walter's bed.

Kendricks saw him pass over. Or he thought he did, anyway. Walter lay there very still and then there was a twitch on his face and a long, deep sigh, and then he was still again but in a different and obviously final way. He had crossed over for sure.

Grace Helms had seen this, too.

For a long time she said nothing. She just held Walter's hand and stared at his face. Then she stood up and took pennies from the pocket of her muslin apron and put them on his eyes.

"It's time for you to go now, Mr. Kendricks," she said.

He started to talk but she stopped him.

"You know there's nothing to say, Mr. Kendricks, and so do I. So I'd appreciate if you got on your horse and rode."

There were so many things in her—anger, grief, melancholy—things he wanted to speak to somehow. But as she'd said, there was nothing to say.

By dawn, dry and golden in the east, he was three miles past the Helms place and riding fast to nowhere in particular.

Dance Girl

AT THE TIME of her murder, Madge Tucker had been living in Cedar Rapids, two blocks west of the train depot, for seven years.

After several quick interviews with other boarders in the large frame rooming house, investigating officers learned that Madge Evelyn Tucker had first come to the city from a farm near Holbrook in 1883. At the time she'd been seventeen years old. After working as a clerk in a millinery store, where her soft good looks made her a mark for young suitors in straw boaters and eager smiles, she met a man named Marley who owned four taverns in and around the area of the Star Wagon Company and the Chicago and Northwestern Railyards. She spent the final five years of her life being a dance girl in these places. All this came to an end when someone entered her room on the night of August 14, 1890.

A Dr. Baines, who was substituting for the vacationing doctor the police ordinarily used, brought a most peculiar piece of information to the officer in charge. After examining Madge Evelyn Tucker, he had come to two conclusions—one being that she'd been stabbed twice in the chest and the second being that she had died a virgin.

One did not expect to hear about a dance girl dying a virgin.

Two months later, just as autumn was turning treetops red and gold and brown, a tall, slender young man in a dark Edwardian suit and a Homburg stepped from the early morning Rock

Island train and surveyed the platform about him. He was surrounded by people embracing each other—sons and mothers,
mothers and fathers, daughters and friends. A shadow of
sorrow passed over his dark eyes as he watched this happy
tableau. Then, with a large-knuckled hand, he lifted his
carpetbag and began walking toward the prosperous downtown
area, the skyline dominated by a six-story structure that
housed the Cedar Rapids Savings Bank.

He found a horse-drawn trolley, asked the driver where he
might find a certain cemetery, and sat back and tried to relax as
two plump women discussed the forthcoming election for
mayor.

For the rest of the ride, he read the letters he kept in his suit
coat. The return address was always the same, as was the
name. Madge Evelyn Tucker. Just now, staring at her beautiful
penmanship, tears formed in his eyes. He realized that the two
women who had been arguing about the present mayor had
stopped talking and were staring at him.

Rather than face their scrutiny, he got off the trolley at the
next block and walked the remaining distance to the cemetery.

He wondered, an hour and a half later, if he had not come to
Cedar Rapids on the worst sort of whim. Perhaps his grief over
his dead sister Madge was undoing him. Hadn't Mr. Staley at
the bank where Richard Tucker worked suggested a "leave of
absence"? What he'd meant, of course, was that Richard was
behaving most strangely and that good customers were becoming upset.

Now Richard crouched behind a wide oak tree. In the early
October morning, the sky pure blue, a chicken hawk looping
and diving against this blue, Richard smelled grass burning in
the last of the summer sun and heard the song of jays and
bluebirds and the sharp resonating bass of distant prowling
dogs.

It would be so pleasant just to sit here uphill from the place where she'd been buried. Just sit here and think of her as she'd been. . . .

But he had things to do. That was why a Navy Colt trembled in his big hand. That was why his other hand kept touching the letters inside his jacket.

By three P.M. the man had not come. By four P.M. the man had not come. By five P.M. the man had not come.

Richard began to grow even more nervous, hidden behind the oak and looking directly down at his sister's headstone. Perhaps the man had come very early in the morning, before Richard's arrival. Or perhaps the man wasn't coming at all.

A rumbling wagon of day workers from a construction site came past the iron cemetery fence, bringing dust and the smell of beer and the cheer of their worn-out laughter with them. Later, a stage coach, one of the few remaining in service anywhere in the Plains states, jerked and jostled past, a solitary passenger looking bored with it all. Finally, a young man and woman on sparkling new bicycles came past the iron fence. He saw in the gentle lines of the woman's face Madge's own gentle lines.

I tried to warn you, Madge.

His remembered words shook him. All his warnings. All his pleadings. For nothing. Madge, good sweet Madge, saw nothing wrong in being a dance girl, not if you kept, as she always said, "your virtue."

Well, the doctor had said at her death that her virtue had indeed remained with her.

But virtue hadn't protected her from the night of August 14. It hadn't protected her at all.

Dusk was chill. Early stars shone in the gray-blue firmament. The distant dogs now sounded lonely.

Crouched behind the oak, Richard pulled his collar up and began blowing on his hands so the knuckles would not feel so raw. Below, the graveyard had become a shadowy place, the tips of granite headstones white in the gloom.

Several times he held his Ingram watch up to the light of the half-moon. He did this at five-minute intervals. The last time, he decided he would leave if nothing happened in the next five minutes.

The man appeared just after Richard had finished consulting his watch.

He was a short man, muscular, dressed in a suit and wearing a Western-style hat. At the cemetery entrance, he looked quickly about, as if he sensed he were being spied upon, and then moved without hesitation to Madge's headstone.

The roses he held in his hand were put into an empty vase next to the headstone. The man then dropped to his knees and made a large and rather dramatic sign of the cross.

He was so involved in his prayers that he did not even turn around until Richard was two steps away. By then it was too late.

Richard shot the man three times in the back of the head— the man who had never been charged with the murder of Richard's sister.

On the train that night, Richard took out the letter in which Madge had made reference to the man in the cemetery. Cletus Boyer, the man's name had been. He'd been a clerk in a haberdasher's and was considered quite a ladies' man.

He met Madge shortly after she became a dance girl. He made one terrible mistake. He fell in love with her. He begged her to give up the taverns but she would not. This only seemed to make his love the more unbearable for him.

He began following her, harassing her, and then he began slapping her.

Finally, Madge gave up the dance hall. By now, she realized how much Cletus loved her. She had grown, in her way, to love him. She took a job briefly with Greene's Opera House. Cletus was to take her home to meet his parents, prominent people on the east side. But over the course of the next month, Madge saw that for all he loved her, he could never accept her past as a dance girl. He pleaded with her to help him in some way—he did not want to feel the rage and shame that boiled up in him whenever he thought of her in the arms of other men. But not even her assurances that she was still a virgin helped. Thinking of her as a dance girl threatened his sanity.

All these things were told Richard in the letter. One more thing was added.

Whenever he called her names and struck her, he became paralyzed with guilt. He brought her gifts of every sort by way of apology. "I don't know what to do, Brother. He is so complicated and tortured a man." Finally, she broke off with him and went back to the taverns.

As the train rattled through the night, the Midwestern plains silver in the dew and moonlight, Richard Tucker sat now feeling sorry for the man he'd just killed.

Richard supposed that in his way Cletus Boyer really had loved Madge.

He sighed, glancing at the letter again.

The passage about Cletus bringing gifts of apology had proved to Richard that Boyer was a sentimental man. And a sentimental killer, Richard had reasoned, was likely to become especially sentimental on the day of a loved one's birthday. That was how Richard had known that Cletus would come to the cemetery today. A sentimental killer.

Richard put the letter away and looked out again at the silver prairie, hoarfrost and pumpkins on the horizon line. A dread came over him as he thought of his job in the bank and the little furnished room where he lived. He felt suffocated now. In the end, his life would come to nothing, just as his sister's life had come to nothing, just as Cletus Boyer's life had come to nothing. There had been a girl once but now there was a girl no longer. There had been the prospect of a better job once, but these days he was too tired to pursue one. Dragging himself daily to the bank was easier—

The prairie rushed past. And the circle of moon, ancient and secret and indifferent, stood still.

The world was a senseless place, Richard knew as the train plunged onward into the darkness. A senseless place.

Deathman

T HE NIGHT before he killed a man, Hawes always followed the same ritual.

He arrived in town late afternoon—in this case, a chill shadowy autumn afternoon—found the best hotel, checked in, took a hot bath in a big metal tub, put on a fresh suit so dark it hinted at the ministerial, buffed his black boots till they shone, and then went down to the lobby in search of the best steak in town.

Because this was a town he'd worked many times before, he knew just which restaurant to choose, a place called "Ma's Gaslight Inn." Ma had died last year of a venereal disease (crazed as hell, her friends said, in her last weeks, talking to dead people and drawing crude pictures of her tombstone again and again on the wall next to her death bed.)

Dusk and chill rain sent townspeople scurrying for home, the clatter of wagons joining the clop of horses in retreat from the small, prosperous mountain town.

Hawes strode the boardwalk alone, a short and burly man handsome except for his acne-pitted cheeks. Even in his early forties, his boyhood taint was obvious.

Rain dripped in fat silver beads from the overhangs as he walked down the boardwalk toward the restaurant. He liked to look in the shop windows when they were closed this way, look at the female things—a lace shawl, a music box with a ballerina dancing atop, a ruby necklace so elegant it looked as if it had been plucked from the fat white neck of a duchess only moments ago.

Without his quite wanting them to, all these things reminded him of Sara. Three years they'd been married until she'd learned his secret, and then she'd been so repelled she invented a reason to visit her mother back in Ohio, and never again returned. He was sure she had remarried—he'd received divorce papers several years ago—and probably even had children by now. Children—and a house with a creek in back—had been her most devout wish.

He quit looking in the shop windows. He now looked straight ahead. His boot heels were loud against the wet boards. The air smelled cold and clean enough to put life in the lungs of the dead.

The player piano grew louder the closer to the restaurant he got; and then laughter and the clink of glasses.

Standing there, outside it all, he felt a great loneliness, and now when he thought of Sara he was almost happy. Having even sad memories was better than no memories at all.

He walked quickly to the restaurant door, pushed it open and went inside.

He needed to be with people tonight.

He was halfway through his steak dinner (fat pats of butter dripping golden down the thick sides of the meat and potatoes sliced and fried in tasty grease) when the tall man in the gray suit came over.

At this time the restaurant was full, low-hanging Rochester lamps casting small pools of light into the ocean of darkness. Tobacco smoke lay a haze over everything, seeming to muffle conversations. An old Negro stood next to the double doors of the kitchen, filling water glasses and handing them to the big-hipped waitresses hurrying in and out the doors. The rest of the house was packed with the sort of people you saw in mining towns—wealthy miners and wealthy men who managed the mines for eastern bosses; and hard, scrubbed-clean working men with their hard, scrubbed-clean wives out celebrating a birthday or an anniversary at the place where the rich folks dine.

"Excuse me."

Hawes looked up. "Yes?"

"I was wondering if you remembered me."

Hawes looked him over. "I guess."

"Good. Then you mind if I sit down?"

"You damn right I do. I'm eating."

"But last time you promised that—"

Hawes dismissed the man with a wave of a pudgy hand. "Didn't you hear me? I'm eating. And I don't want to be interrupted."

"Then after you're finished eating—?"

Hawes shrugged. "We'll see. Now get out of here and leave me alone."

The man was very young, little more than a kid, twenty-one, twenty-two at most, and now he seemed to wither under the assault of Hawes' intentional and practiced rudeness.

"I'll make sure you're done eating before I bother you again."

Hawes said nothing. His head was bent to the task of cutting himself another piece of succulent steak.

The tall man went away.

"It's me again. Richard Sloane."

"So I see."

The tall man looked awkward. "You're smoking a cigar."

"So I am."

"So I take it you're finished eating?"

Hawes almost had to laugh, the sonofabitch looked so young and nervous. They weren't making them tough, the way they'd been in the frontier days. "I suppose I am."

"Then may I sit down?"

Hawes pointed a finger at an empty chair. The young man sat down.

"You know what I want?" He took out a pad and pencil the way any good journalist would.

"Same thing you people always want."

"How it feels after you do it."

Hawes smiled. "You mean do I feel guilty? Do I have nightmares?"

The young man looked uncomfortable with Hawes' playful tone. "I guess that's what I mean, yes."

Hawes stared at the young man.

"You ever seen one, son?"

The youngster looked as if he was going to object to "son" but then changed his mind. "Two. One when I was a little boy with my uncle and one last year."

"Did you like it?"

"I hated it. It scared me the way people acted, it made me sick. They were—celebrating. It was like a party."

"Yes, some of them get that way sometimes."

Hawes had made a study of it all so he considered telling Sloane here about Tom Galvin, an Irishman of the sixteenth century who had personally hanged more than 1,600 men. Galvin believed in giving the crowd a show, especially with men accused of treason. These he not only hanged but oftentimes dismembered, throwing arms and legs to the crazed onlookers. Some reports had it that some of the crowds actually ate of the bloodied limbs tossed to them.

"You ever hang two at once?"

"The way they did in Nevada last year?" Hawes smirked and shook his head. "Not me, son. I'm not there to put on a show. I'm there to kill a man." He took a drag on his cigar. "I don't want to give my profession a bad name."

God knew that executioners, as a group, were unreliable. In

seventeenth-century England, the executioner himself was put in a jail cell for eight days preceding the hanging—so officials would know he'd show up on time and sober.

"Will you sleep well tonight?"

"Very well, I hope."

"You won't think about tomorrow?"

"Not very seriously."

"How the man will look?"

"No."

"Or how the trap will sound when it opens?"

"No."

"Or how his eyes will bulge and his tongue will bloat?"

Hawes shook his head. "I know what you want, son. You want a speech about the terrible burden of being an executioner." He tapped his chest. "But I don't have it in me."

"Then it isn't a burden?"

"No, son, it isn't. It's just what I do. The way some men milk cows and other men fix buggies—I hang people. It's just that simple."

The young man looked disappointed. They always did when Hawes told them this. They wanted melodrama—they wanted regret and remorse and a tortured soul.

Hawes decided to give him the story about the woman. It wasn't the whole story, of course, but the part he always told was just what frontier newspapermen were looking for.

"There was a blonde woman once."

"Blonde?"

"So blonde it almost hurt your eyes to look at her hair in the sunlight. It was spun gold."

"Spun gold; God."

"And it was my duty to hang her."

"Oh, shit."

"The mayor of the town said I'd be hanging a woman but I never dreamt she'd be so beautiful."

"Did you hang her anyway?"

"I had to, son. It's my job."

"Did she cry?"

"She was strong. She didn't cry and her legs didn't give out when she was climbing the scaffold stairs. You know, I've seen big strapping men just collapse on those stairs and have to be carried all the way up. And some of them foul their pants. I can smell the stench when I'm pulling the white hood over their eyes."

"But she was strong?"

"Very strong. She walked right over to the trap door and stood on top of it and folded her hands very primly in front of her. And then she just waited for me to come over there."

"What was she guilty of?"

"She'd taken a lover that spring, and when her husband found out he tried to kill her. But instead she killed him. The jury convicted her of first-degree murder."

"It doesn't sound like first-degree to me."

"Me either, son. But I'm the hangman; I'm not the judge."

"And so you hanged her?"

"I did."

"Didn't you want to call it off?"

"A part of me did."

"Did she scream when the door dropped away?"

"She didn't say anything."

"And her neck snapped right away?"

"I made sure of that, son. I didn't want her to dangle there and strangle the way they sometimes do. So I cinched the knot extra tight. She crossed over right away. You could hear her neck break."

"This was how many years ago?"

"Ten."

"And obviously you still think about her."

It was clear now the angle the young journalist would be

taking. Hangman kills beautiful woman; can't get her out of his mind these long years later. His readers would love it.

"Oh, yes, son; yes, I still think about her."

The excitement was plain on the man's young face. Hangman kills beautiful woman, can't forget her. This may just have been the best story he'd ever had.

He flipped the cover of his pad closed. "I really appreciate this."

Hawes nodded.

The young man got up, snatched his derby from the edge of the table, and walked to the rear where the press of people and smoke and clatter were overwhelming.

Hawes took the time for another two drinks and half a Cuban cigar and then went out into the rain.

The house was three blocks away, in the opposite direction of the gallows, for which Hawes was grateful. A superstitious man, he believed that looking at a gallows the night before would bring bad luck. The man would not die clean, the trap would not open, the rope would mysteriously snap—something. And so he didn't glimpse the gallows until the morning of the execution.

Hawes came this way often. This town was in the exact center of the five-hundred-mile radius he traveled as an executioner. So he came to this town three or four times a month, not just when he had somebody to hang here.

And he always came to Maude's.

Maude was the plump giggling madam who ran the town's only whorehouse. She had an agreement with the sheriff that if she kept her house a quarter mile away from town, and if she ran her place clean, meaning no black whores or no black customers, then the sheriff would leave her alone, meaning of course he would keep at bay the zealous German Lutherans who mostly made up the town. Maude gave the lawman money but not much, and every once in awhile he'd sneak up on the back porch where one of the runaway farm girls she employed would offer the sheriff her wet glistening lips.

He could hear the player piano now, Hawes could, lonely on the rainy prairie night. He wished he hadn't told that pipsqueak journalist about the blonde woman because now Hawes was thinking about her again, and what had really happened that morning.

The house was a white two-story frame. In front, two horses were tied to a post, and down a ways a buggy dun stood ground-tied.

Hawes went up to the door and knocked.

Maude herself opened it. "Well, for shit's sake, girls, look who's here."

Downstairs there was a parlor, which was where the player piano was, and the girls sat on a couch and you chose them the way you did cattle at a livestock auction.

Hawes always asked for the same one. He looked at the five girls sitting there watching him. They were about what you'd expect for a midwestern prairie whorehouse, young girls quickly losing their bloom. They drank too much and laughed too loud and weren't always good about keeping themselves clean.

That was why he always asked for Lucy.

"She here, Maude?"

Maude winked at him. "Just taking a bath."

"I see."

"Won't be long." She knew his tastes, knew he didn't want to stay downstairs with the girls and the piano and the two cowboys who were giggling about which girls they'd pick. "You know the end room on the hall?"

"Right."

"Why don't you go up there and wait for her?"

"Good idea."

"You'll find some bourbon in the drawer."

"Appreciate it."

She winked at him again. "Hear you're hanging the Parsons boy in the morning."

"I never know their names."

"Well, take it from me, sweetie, when he used to come here he didn't tip worth a damn. Anything he gets from you, he's got coming." And then she whooped a laugh and slapped him on the back and said, "You just go right up those stairs, sweetie."

He nodded, mumbling a thank you, and turned away from her before he had to look directly at the small brown stubs of her teeth. The sight and stench of her mouth had always sickened him.

He wondered how many men had lain in this dark room. He wondered how many men had felt his loneliness. He wondered how many men had heard a woman's footsteps coming down the hall, and felt fear and shame.

Lucy opened the door. She was silhouetted in the flickering hall light. "You want me to get a lantern?"

"That's all right."

She laughed. "Never known a man who likes the dark the way you do."

She came in, closed the door behind her. She smelled of soapy bath water and jasmine. She wasn't pretty but she kept herself clean and he appreciated it.

"Should've just left my clothes off, I guess," she said. "After my bath, I mean."

He could tell she was nervous. The darkness always made her like this.

Wind and rain spattered against the window. The fingers of a dead branch scraped the glass, a curious kind of music.

She came over to the bed and stood above him. She took his hand and pressed it lightly against her sex. She was dry and warm.

"You going to move over?"

He rolled over so there was room for her. He lay on his back and stared at the ceiling.

As usual when they lay there, Lucy smoked a cigarette. She always hand-rolled two or three before coming to see Hawes because many times the night consisted of talk and nothing more.

"You want a drag?"

"No, thanks."

"How you doing?"

"All right, I guess."

"Hear you're going to hang a man tomorrow."

"Yes."

Next to him, she shuddered, her whole naked skinny body. "Forgive me for saying so, Hawes, but I just don't know how you can do it."

"You've said that before."

She laughed again. "Yes, I guess I have."

They lay there silent for a time, just the wind and the rain pattering the roof, just the occasional glow of her cigarette as she dragged on it, just his own breathing.

And the darkness; oh, yes, the darkness.

"You ever read anything by Louisa May Alcott?" Lucy asked.

"No."

"I'm reading this book by her now. It's real good, Hawes, you should read it sometime."

"Maybe I will."

That was another thing he liked about Lucy. Where most of the girls were ignorant, Lucy had gone through fourth grade before running away, and had learned to read. Hawes could carry on a good conversation with her and he appreciated that. Of course, she was older too, twenty-five or so, and that also made a difference.

They fell into silence again.

After awhile he rolled over and kissed her.

She said, "Just a minute."

She stubbed her cigarette out and then rolled back to him and then they got down to it seriously.

The fear was there as always—could he actually do it and do it right without humiliating himself?—but tonight he had no trouble.

He was good and hard and he got into her with no trouble and she responded as if she really gave a damn about him, and then he climaxed and collapsed next to her, his breath heaving in the darkness, feeling pretty damn good about himself as a man again.

She didn't say anything for a long time there in the wind and rain and darkness, smoking a cigarette again, and then she said, "That's why she left you, isn't it?"

"Huh?"

"Your wife. Why she left you."

"I'm not following you." But he was in fact following her and he sensed that she was going to say something he didn't want to hear.

"That time you got drunk up here in the room."

"Yeah? What about it?"

"You told me about your wife leaving you."

"So?"

"But you wouldn't tell me *why* she left you. You just kept saying 'She had a good reason, I guess.' Well, I finally figured out what that reason is."

He was silent for a time again, and so was she.

Obviously she could sense that she'd spooked him and now she was feeling bad about it. "I shouldn't have said anything, Hawes. I'm sorry."

"It's all right."

He was feeling the loneliness again. He wanted to cry but he wasn't a man given to tears.

"Me and my big mouth," Lucy said, lighting another cigarette.

In the flash of flame, he could see her face. Soft, freckled, eyes the blue of a spring sky.

They lay in silence a long time.

She said, "You angry at me, Hawes?"

"No."

"I'm sorry I said anything."

"I know."

"I mean, it doesn't bother me. The way you are."

"I know."

"It's kind of funny, even."

"It isn't funny to me."

And it hadn't been funny to his wife, Sara, either. Once she figured out the pattern, she'd left him immediately.

"How'd you figure it out?" he asked.

"I just started keeping track."

"Oh."

"But I won't tell anybody. I mean, if that's what's bothering you."

"I appreciate it. You keeping it to yourself, I mean."

"You can't help the way you are."

"No; no, I guess I can't."

He thought of how angry and disgusted his wife Sara had been when she'd finally understood that he was impotent all the time except for the night before a hanging. Only then could he become fully a man.

The snap of the trap door; the snap of the neck. And then extinction. Blackness; utter, eternal blackness. And Hawes controlling it all.

In the wind and darkness, she said, "You ever think about how it'll be for you personally?"

"How what'll be?"

"Death."

"Yeah; I guess so."

"You think there're angels?"

"No."

"You think there's a heaven?"

"No."

"You think there's a God?"

"No."

She took a long drag on her cigarette. "Neither do I, Hawes. But I sure wish I did."

From down the hall, Hawes could hear a man laughing, then a woman joining in. The player piano downstairs was going again.

"Would you just hold me?" Hawes said.

"What?"

"Just hold me in your arms."

"Sure."

"Real tight."

"All right."

She stubbed out her cigarette and then rolled back to him.

She took him in her arms with surprising tenderness, and held him to her, her soft breasts warm against his chest, and then she said, "Sometimes, I think you're my little boy, Hawes. You know that?"

But Hawes wasn't paying attention; he was listening to the chill rain on the dark wind, and the lonely frantic laughter down the hall.

The wind grew louder then, and Lucy fell silent, just holding him tighter; tighter.

Love and Trooper Monroe

UNTIL MONROE started killing rattlesnakes, nobody had ever paid him much attention.

Monroe was a pudgy, twenty-three-year-old recruit from Ohio. He had been with the U.S. Cavalry four years now, usually working at the tasks the Captain gave only to those troops he didn't consider important.

Such as killing rattlers.

C Company had been a dusty month on the march and had two days ago worked its way down mountainous hills to a valley bright with a silver river and sweet with cottonwood trees. The area met the Army's qualifications for a proper camping ground: wood, water and good ground.

C Company needed a rest and Captain Lionel Marsh knew it and so he instructed his men to put in here several days.

Everything was fine. The valley offered antelope, elk, buffalo, wild turkey, black-tailed deer, wild goose, plover and duck. There were even wild bullberries, from which you could make simple jelly, which went especially well with turkey.

The Captain slept in his wik-a-up. He cut some willow saplings, stuck them straight up in the ground, wove the ends loosely together on top, then threw two saddle blankets over the top. He had his own little apartment, which was where he spent the entire night, with troopers standing guard till dawn. (Regulation tents were available to the Captain of course; he just felt hardier adopting the methods of the plains Indians.)

The other troopers weren't so lucky. They had to sleep on the ground, and because of the river, which had been at flood levels not so long ago, rattlesnakes were everywhere. Nobody wanted to fall asleep with poisonous vipers crawling around in the darkness.

So after dinner, four men, including Monroe, were dispatched to cut and tear away reeds and grass, and to beat the ground with long sticks that resembled knotty Irish walking canes, so as to drive the snakes away.

They killed as many as possible, and Monroe proved to be the best of the four. Some he shot; some he stomped on with his heel, shattering their heads; some he crushed with big rocks that he dropped like bombs.

A young Kentucky recruit, fascinated by all this snake-killing, stood close by keeping count. After the four men had returned to the light and warmth of the campfire, the kid from Kentucky claimed that Monroe had killed sixteen rattlers, far more than any of the others.

And so for the first time, many of the more important men became aware of Monroe. They congratulated him across the flickering fire, and said with all genuine humility that they sure as hell wouldn't want to have to kill rattlers, what a hell of a job that would be, and Monroe was one brave and inspiring cuss all right.

But it wasn't the officers Monroe wanted congratulations from.

On this seven-week march to a fort on the farthest frontier, the Captain had seen fit to bring his nineteen-year-old daughter Mae. She wore not the gingham dresses and bonnets of the day but rather the corded pants and cotton shirts of day workers. Nor was there any beauty to be found in her face, which was round and very nearly ugly; nor her body, which was, to be kind, thirty pounds overweight, with none of the excess distributed in any fetching way at all.

To most of C Company she was every bit as invisible as Monroe himself, and it was this very fact that caused Monroe to fall in love with her. It was his feeling that he had at last met the woman who was proper for him, to whom he would pledge his love, whom he would ask for children, and whose cool hand would lay on his fevered forehead when death came sometime in the unimaginable future.

But if Mae sensed any of this, she certainly didn't let on.

Many times Monroe had gone up to her to offer a hand with her saddle, or an extra ax with firewood, or an extra cup of water when she stood baking in the hot afternoon sunlight. But at these times, even if she muttered a thank you for his offer, she seemed unable to bring him into any focus, as if he wasn't quite there at all. Just the way most of C Company treated him.

He wanted to take her and shake her by the shoulders and say: *Don't you know we're fated? Don't you know I lie next to the campfire at night dreaming of how you'll look in your white wedding dress? Don't you know that we'll have a family together?*

But it was sadly clear to him that she understood none of these things and that was why he developed the idea for rescuing her.

Monroe loved to read the yellowback novels wherein lowborn young men cadged themselves dreamy wives by rescuing them from some terrible fate—the sinking canoe, the runaway horse, the lustful clutches of the dastard.

And that was just what he planned to do in the morning when Mae, as always, took some of the cooking utensils down to the river bank to scour with sand and water.

Dinner that night consisted of what was called sonofabitch stew, a young calf slaughtered to render not just beef but a stew that consisted of cut-up heart, testicles, tongue, liver and marrow gut, and which some, though not all, considered a treat.

"You men, goodnight," Mae said, standing on the edge of the fireglow.

They answered in ragged chorus, officers and enlisted men alike, "Good night, Miss," all except for Monroe, who waited till the others had finished.

And then his Good Night rose like a piece of music above the mutter of the men, above the shush of the river and the call of the coyotes and the banter of night birds, "Good night, Mae; good night."

And he knew there were tears in his eyes because all his life, and a hardscrabble farmboy life it had been, he'd waited to feel not simply the coarse urgency of lust but the gentle noble warmth of true love. As in the songs of Stephen Foster and a hundred yellowback novels.

He would set a rattler on her tomorrow, and then rescue her at the last terrible moment, and then she would have no choice but to look, to really look, at the young man who'd saved her, the young man she would then love forever.

Monroe spent the first part of the morning with the horses. When they were in the fort, the soldiers of C Company spent an hour in the morning and an hour in the afternoon grooming their animals. The Army wanted man and horse to function as one, and indeed some men became so attached to their animals that they managed to keep the same animal for the full five years of enlistment. On march, it fell to men like Monroe to keep the horses healthy and reasonably clean and content.

Around nine-thirty, the heat of the day still stinking of breakfast smoke, Monroe saw Mae, dressed in her usual costume of corded trousers and cotton workshirt, start gathering up pans and taking them down to the riverbank, where she squatted next to the swift blue water and scrubbed out the metal insides with rags and sand.

Monroe let her make three trips and then he moved, dropping the currycomb to the ground, walking quickly down near the water.

He didn't have to wonder where he'd find a rattler.

There was a thick undergrowth twenty feet to the right of where Mae squatted. Hit the growth with his stick and a rattler was guaranteed to appear.

He hadn't planned on being scared.

He felt like some kind of criminal. He felt as if everybody was staring at him.

But it would be worth it.

Soon, Mae would not only know of his love for her; she would realize her love for him.

Mae sang a Stephen Foster song. She had a high, almost fragile voice, one every bit as lovely as the sunlight golden on the surface of the river.

He looked upslope, to make sure nobody was watching. Then he looked to the river again to make certain that Mae was properly busy with her pots and pans.

Satisfied that now was the proper time, he began beating the undergrowth with his stick.

In moments, a rattler appeared, a timber rattlesnake, stretching maybe five feet in length as it wriggled angrily from beneath the prickly gray bushes, the numerous rings of old skin on the molting indicating that this was an older fellow, the loose, horny rattle at the end of the tail already making deadly noise.

Monroe knew he had to be damned careful. This wasn't going to be an easy one to pick up.

But, knowing that at any moment another trooper could walk down here, and knowing that at any moment Mae could get up and leave, he leaned down quickly, feinted to the left and then jerked abruptly back, faking the snake into striking in the wrong direction, grabbing the rattler safely behind the head.

The thing wriggled and rattled and Monroe wondered for a terrible moment if it might not jump from his grasp.

Now he had to move even more quickly, to within ten feet or so of Mae, where he'd drop the rattler on the ground and shout for her to watch out. Then he'd kill the rattler and be her hero.

He flung the snake.

It tumbled in the air twice, slow-motion, before landing.

But as it started to reach the ground, Monroe saw that he had underestimated the reach of the snake. It would land only a foot or so from Mae.

Even before the snake touched down, Monroe cupped his hands and shouted "Mae! Mae!"

But by the time she turned, it was too late.

The rattler hissed, then struck her in the arm just as the startled Mae turned to see what Trooper Monroe was yelling about.

He would never forget the look on her face at that moment: confusion and fear as she turned to see the rattler arcing toward her, then shock as the snake implanted its venom through its long, hollow teeth.

"Mae!" Monroe cried, running toward her. "Mae!" he shouted as the snake, satisfied, undulated its way to the relative safety of the underbrush.

By nightfall, two different types of medical attention had been visited upon Mae. Originally, the Captain opted for cutting the wound open and sucking the venom out. But later in the day a master sergeant convinced the Captain that granny medicine was worth trying, and so the bite was dowsed with kerosene and live chicken flesh was used to supposedly draw even more of the venom out.

Now, near night, Mae lay in a tent, the light of a kerosene lantern flickering across the walls.

The men had been thunderstruck by Mae's wound. It was all they talked about at dinner, and afterward they hovered near her tent, shaking their heads and saying silent prayers. To Army regulars, the Captain's daughter had represented both good humor and a certain sense of democracy. She'd been cordial with them all.

Monroe just stared into the fire.

He hadn't eaten lunch or dinner.

Every few minutes he'd raise his head and look past the edge of the campfire to the tent where Mae was.

He still could not believe he could have been so reckless.

He still could not believe that the snake had actually struck her.

"You all right?" the sergeant said after coming back from the bushes where he'd taken his nightly purging.

"Yessir."

"You didn't hunt them snakes down tonight."

"No, sir."

"Why not?"

"Feelin' sickly, I guess."

The sergeant said, "Expect you to be huntin' them snakes tomorrow night."

"Yessir."

An hour later, most of the company turned in. Soon men were snoring and whispering things to themselves in their sleep.

Monroe had gotten into his sleeping roll but he was anything but asleep. He just kept thinking of Mae. Of how much he loved her. Of what a fool he'd been.

Around midnight there was a wail, a distinctive sound a man makes when he's been overcome with sorrow. The sound came from the Captain's tent.

He did not have to wonder who had made the sound, or why.

A few minutes later, there came weeping, weeping so unabashed it sounded as if the Captain would never recover.

And then there was silence. Plain, awful silence.

Around two, the campfire guttering, everybody else seemingly asleep, Monroe slipped out of his bedroll and headed down for the riverbank.

He didn't put his boots on. He didn't need them anymore.

In the moonlight, the river was silver and curiously quiet now.

Monroe lay down on the bank, just where Mae had been this morning, not far at all from the underbrush and the rattlers.

He didn't have long to wait.

Nor did he move, not even give the slightest jerk, when the snake was upon him, filling his veins with venom.

Oh, Mae, he thought; oh, Mae.

In the morning they found him just where she'd been, the body of him anyway.

The spirit of him was elsewhere, perhaps at last with his one true love's.

Pards

Bromley always liked it when people asked him what he did for a living because then he could tell them he was a writer. He didn't mention his day job, which was being the only forty-nine-year-old bag "boy" at DeSoto's Supermarket; no, he just told them about his writing, and then showed them a copy of the one and only paperback novel he'd ever sold, a western called *Gun Fury*, which had been published by a company called Triton. He never mentioned that Triton had declared bankruptcy right after *Gun Fury* appeared, nor did he mention that Triton had been one of the worst publishers in history. Bromley's listeners didn't need to know that.

2

"Never seen anything like these before," the new mailman said on one of Bromley's days off (he usually worked week-ends, which most of the teenagers refused to do, and so Sam DeSoto gave him two days off in the middle of the week). Bromley was sitting on the front porch of the aged Victorian apartment house where he lived, reading William Nolan's biography of Max Brand and sipping on a Diet Pepsi. In addition to losing his hair, Bromley had lately started to gain weight, one of the Chicano kids at the store even calling him

"Fat Ass" one day, the little bastard, and so now it was Diet Pepsi instead of the regular stuff.

So Bromley was in the shade of the sunny porch, Mrs. Hanrahan's soap opera blaring through the lacy curtains, when the mailman said, "What exactly are they, anyway?"

"Fanzines."

"Fanzines?"

"Yeah, magazines that western fans publish themselves. There're fanzines for people who like the old pulp magazines and fanzines for people who liked the old Saturday serials and fanzines for people who like the old western stars."

The mailman, who was just old enough to remember, said, "Like Gene and Roy?"

"Exactly. Like Gene and Roy."

"So do you put one out yourself, I mean being a writer and all?"

"No; but I write for a lot of them."

"Yeah? Which ones?"

"The ones about the old cowboy stars." Bromley wanted to tell him about his dream he had sometimes; standing in this movie lobby in 1948 with all these great lobby cards showing Wild Bill Elliott and The Durango Kid (God, there was no getting around it; guys who wore masks were just great) and Gabby Hayes and Jane Frazee and Tim Holt and The 3 Mesquiteers, and how down on one end there was this table overflowing with pulp magazines, *The Pecos Kid Western* and *Frontier Stories* and *Thrilling Western Stories*; and then another table with an old 1946 table model radio with the sounds of "Bobby Benson and The B Bar B Riders" coming out of it; and yet another table with nothing but Big Little Books; and there was a church-like holiness in the air and Bromley was caught up in it, tears nearly streaming down his face; WAS NOT THIS HEAVEN? And he had this crazy urge to eat Cheerios, just the way Tonto did; or Ralston Purina, just like Tom Mix; or maybe even Pep, the way Superman was always telling him to.

"Those'd be the ones I'd be interested in, the cowboys, I mean," the mailman said. Then he shrugged and handed Bromley his mail. "You're really an interesting guy, Ken, you know that?"

3

He'd been married once, Bromley had, in the early sixties, already working at DeSoto's, to a pretty but dumb woman whom his mother did not like at all ("I don't see why you have to move out when you've got so much room here, especially since your father died, and anyway twenty-two is too young to get married, she's just looking for an easy ride if you ask me"), a waitress who seemed to know what all her customers made per hour at this-or-that factory, at this-or-that delivery service. "Four bucks an hour, Ken, you really should look into that." But somehow he never got around to it. Just down the block from DeSoto's was the city's largest used bookstore and he spent most of his lunch hours in there. The air was holy, the dusty air of Ace Doubles and Gold Medal books, of *All-Story Weekly* and *Star Western* and *Adventure*, the cocoon of paperbacks and magazines in which he'd spent his boyhood, never much caring that he didn't have many friends, that he was virtually invisible at school, or that the violent arguments of his parents caused him to shake uncontrollably for long periods of time behind his too-thin bedroom door. No, there were always the Saturday afternoon movies, or his books and magazines to escape into.

One night—this was a year or so into their marriage, the night one of those perfect late spring evenings shot through with fireflies and the scent of apple blossoms—right there in the same wedding bed Bromley would sleep in the rest of his life, right there in Mrs. Hanrahan's apartment house where he would live the rest of his life, his wife said, "I need to be honest with you."

"Huh?"

"I—did something."

"Did something?"

He was smoking a Lucky with the sheet just half on him and listening to the night birds at the window screen, and she was lying next to him in just her underwear.

"You know that Jimmy I told you about?"

"Uh, I guess so." She was always telling him about somebody.

"You know. He makes six-thirty-two an hour out at Rockwell."

"I guess."

"He has the red Olds convertible, remember, with the white leather interior?"

"Oh. Yeah. Jimmy."

"Well the other day he wanted to know if I wanted a ride home after the dinner rush."

"Oh."

God, now he knew what was coming.

"I knew I shouldn't have said yes but he kept pushing the subject. You know how guys get."

"Yeah, I guess I do."

"Well, anyway, I let him give me a ride home."

"Was this Thursday?"

"Yeah. Thursday."

"When you were late?"

She hesitated. "Yeah, when I was late."

"I see."

Neither of them said anything for a long time. He finished

his cigarette and then just lay with his hands on his chest, in his boxer shorts which she was always asking him not to wear ("You're a young man, Ken, you shouldn't wear things like that").

Then she said, "But he didn't take me straight home."

"I see."

"I mean I told him to. But he didn't. He wouldn't listen to anything I said. He just kept driving out along the river road. He just kept saying isn't it pretty at dusk like this, with the sunlight real coppery on the river like this? I had to admit that it was."

"Did you let him do anything to you?"

"I let him French kiss me."

"Oh."

"And I let him feel my breasts."

"I see."

"But I didn't let him put his hand inside my bra."

He said nothing. He wondered if his heart would stop beating. Just *boom* like that and he would no longer be alive.

"And I didn't let him touch me down there."

He said nothing.

"He tried, Ken, but I wouldn't let him."

The tears came abruptly and without warning. There in the darkness he shook so hard—just the way he used to shake when his parents screamed at each other—that the whole bed shook. His wedding bed.

She leaned over and kissed him then, and it was a tender and pure kiss, and he recognized it as such, and she said, "You're more like my brother or something, Ken. I didn't want it to turn out this way but it did anyway. I mean you never want to go dancing or take me out to dinner or make love or—" She smiled there in the darkness. "You're more interested in your book collection than you are me, Ken. And you know that's the truth."

Later on after a long time of not talking, just lying there, her sometimes taking drags from his cigarette, sometimes not, she leaned over and kissed him and put her hand down there and got him hard, and then they made love with a purity and tenderness that broke his heart because he knew this would be the last time, the very last time, and when it was over and they were just lying there again, she started crying too, soft girl tears there in the darkness, her a girl as he was still a boy, and then just before she fell asleep she said—her only bitter comment during the whole night—"Well, your mother will be relieved anyway. Just don't move back in with her. I care about you too much to see that happen. OK?"

The next day she was packed and gone. Three months later he got proceeding papers from a lawyer in Milwaukee and six months after that he was divorced. Throughout the first year, she wrote him postcards fairly frequently. She mentioned different restaurants she worked at and she mentioned how hot Milwaukee was in the summer and then how cold it was in the winter and then one card she said she was getting married to a guy with a real good job (she didn't mention his name nor did she mention how much he made an hour) and then abruptly the cards stopped except, inexplicably, two Christmases later when she sent him a Christmas card with the snapshot of an infant girl inside. Her first child.

He stayed on at DeSoto's of course, spending his lunch hours at the used bookstore, and he did not move back in with his mother.

4

The odd thing was, Bromley learned about Rex Stone's moving not through one of the fanzines but when somebody at DeSoto's (Laughlin, the smirky guy in the meat department) mentioned that Stone was moving to Center City, a mere eighty miles from the city here: "That fuckin' cowboy guy, you know, the one when we were kids, the one who could make his horse dance up on his hind legs?"

Bromley could scarcely believe it. Sure, he'd known that Rex Stone (a/k/a Walter Sipkins) had been born in this area but who could have guessed that after fifteen years of being a star at Republic (he'd starred in the studio's very last B-western, despite the fact that most film books mistakenly attributed this distinction to Allan "Rocky" Lane)—after fifteen years in movies and ten more in TV (usually in supporting roles but meaty ones), who could have guessed Stone would move back to where he'd come from?

About a month after Laughlin gave Bromley the word, the local paper ran a big photo of Stone in full singing-cowboy get-up holding up a sweet little crippled girl in his arms. The caption read: "Cowboy Star spends sunset years helping others" and the story went on to detail how active Stone had become with Center City civic events. Retired now, he "planned to devote his life to helping all the little 'buckaroos and buckarettes' who need him."

Bromley couldn't believe it. Rex Stone. Only eighty miles from here. Rex Stone. The man he'd always measured himself against. Sure, Bromley liked Hoppy and Roy and Gene and Monte and Lash and Sunset but none of them had compared to Rex because, despite the fact that Rex sang a lot of sappy songs and could make his horse Stormy dance along at the same time, Rex was a *man*. The jaw and the eyes and the big hands and the deep voice told you that. He was a man not in the way of a Saturday afternoon hero but rather in the rough and somewhat mysterious way of, say, Robert Mitchum. That was why, back in the forties and fifties, Rex Stone had not only had a huge kids' following, he'd also managed to snag a major following of young women. (TV people had later tried to cast him as a he-man in a short-lived adventure series called "Bush Pilot" but the series had been on ZIV, and when ZIV went down—the other networks inevitably pushing it out—so did Rex's series).

And now, admittedly paunchier, gray-haired, and jowly, Rex Stone lived only eighty miles away.

5

"Is Mr. Stone there, please?"

"Who the hell is this?" The voice was female and old and accusatory.

Bromley did the only thing he could. He gulped. "Uh, my name is Bromley."

"Who?"

"Bromley."

"Spell it."

"Huh?"

"You deaf? I said spell it."

"B-r-o-m-l-e-y."

"Bromley."

"Yes."

"So just what the hell do you want?"

"I, uh, I'd like to speak to Mr. Stone."

"He's busy."

And with that, she hung up.

6

Six days later:

Dear Rex Stone,

I know that you're probably too busy to answer all your fan mail so let me assure you that while I'm a long time admirer of yours, this letter has to do with a professional matter.

As a published western author (GUN FURY, Triton Books, 1967 and hundreds of articles in western and popular culture magazines), I'd like to interview you for a forthcoming book about western stars of the forties and fifties called: INTO THE SUNSET (Leisure Books).

You may have noticed by my return address that I don't live very far from you. I'd very much like to come up for a day soon, bring my tape recorder, and spend several hours with you discussing your career.

I phoned several days ago but a woman answered and we seemed to have been disconnected or something.

I'd very much like to meet you and help bring your millions of fans up to date on your life. I know that you never attend any of the "Golden Oldie" shows that Gene and Roy and Lash and the others sometimes go to so this would be a particular treat for everybody who has followed your career.

Please let me know your answer at your earliest convenience. Sincerely yours,

Ken Bromley

7

"Who?"

"Rex Stone."

"Who?"

"Rex Stone. Don't you remember, I used to see all his movies?"

"Movies. Hah. Complete waste of time as far as I'm concerned."

And in fact, that had been his mother's opinion all the time Bromley had been growing up, and it was her opinion even now that she was eighty-seven years old and living in a nursing home thanks to the insurance her husband had left her.

But even in a nursing home, she had control of him. She was sort of like the Scarab in one of the old Republic chapter plays. All-knowing. All-seeing. Plus, she had him trained. He always checked with her on anything major, and certainly buying a Trailways ticket was major, even if it was only for eighty miles, even if it was only for a day. She was convinced that she was about to die of a heart attack at any moment and so she wanted him on call twenty-four hours a day. If he wasn't at DeSoto's then he'd better by God be in his apartment. And she certainly didn't like the idea of a trip to Center City.

"Why would you waste your money on him? He doesn't even make movies any more."

"I want to write an article about him."

"Phoo. Article. They don't even pay you for those things. They only paid you $500 for a whole book. Talk about getting cheated. Why, I read that there Stephen King makes twenty million a year. It was right in *People*."

"It'll only be for a day, Mom. That's all."

"A day? You know how long it takes you to die of a heart attack?" She very impressively snapped her fingers. The sound was of twigs snapping.

They were on the veranda, late afternoon. She had a cigarette going and she was sipping a glass of beer. She'd raised enough hell with the nursing home people that they gave into her once every day. One cigarette. One glass of beer.

"I really want to go, Mom. It's real important to me."

How he hated his voice. His groveling. His begging, really. He was fifty, and nearly bald, and two or three of the clubs he belonged to gave him "senior rates."

And here he was pleading with this shriveled up little woman wound inside a black shawl despite the eighty-eight degrees.

"He have a phone?"

"Yes."

"You make sure you leave me that number."

"All right, Mom."

"It's all a waste of time if you ask me."

He leaned over and kissed her cheek. "I love you, Mom."

She snorted smoke through her nostrils and said, "You're more like your father every day."

He knew she didn't mean that as a compliment.

8

"Who?"

"Rex Stone."

"Guess I must be a little young to remember him or something."

"He was really popular."

"Yeah, I imagine."

Bromley caught the kid's sarcasm, of course. Twerp was maybe sixteen or seventeen and had an arm's length of blue tattoos (Bromley's mother had always insisted that a tattoo was a sure sign of the lower classes) and one tiny silver earring (which marked him as a lot less than manly, even if a lot of young men did wear them).

Bromley would've sat with somebody else but this was the 8:30 A.M. Trailways that went to the state capital and so it was packed with lots of old ladies in big summery hats and so there was no place else to sit. This was the last empty seat and the kid had come with it.

"He set an attendance record at the Denver rodeo," Bromley said.

"Oh."

"And in 1949 he came in right behind Roy Rogers as the biggest box office draw."

"1949, huh?" The kid shrugged and looked out the bus window.

Bromley put his head back and closed his eyes. The bus engine made the whole bus tremble. The smell of diesel fuel reminded Bromley of boyhood summers, walking down to the Templar Theater to see all the new Saturday matinee movies. It was easy to recall the smell of theater popcorn, too, and the way the sunlight blinded you when you emerged onto the sidewalk six hours later, and the way summer dusk fell, the birds somehow sad in the summer trees, and the girls you saw sometimes, always a little older than you and always blonde in a showgirl sort of way, and how they made you ache and how vivid and perfect they remained in your daydreams the whole hot school vacation. Not even after Dr. Fitzsimmons had convinced his mother it was just muscle cramps and not polio at all would she let Bromley go to the movies again. Not until the following summer.

After twenty miles, Bromley opened his eyes again.

Next to him, the kid had this earplug in and his whole body was kind of sit-dancing to the music snaking from the transistor in his lap to the plug in his ear.

The way the kid moved around there, moving and grooving he thought it was called, struck Bromley as downright obscene.

Bromley closed his eyes again, and thought of the summer he got those funny aches in his legs and his mother went crazy and said he had polio for sure and lit candles to the Blessed Mother all summer and wouldn't let Bromley go to any movie theaters. She said that this was the number one place for catching polio germs and then she showed him a newspaper photo of a poor little kid inside an iron lung, a photo she always seemed to have handy.

The kid got off way before Center City, and Bromley had the rest of the trip to enjoy by himself. He'd been holding in gas for a long time and it was a pure pleasure to let it go.

9

"Here you go."

"You sure this is the right address?"

"Center Grove, right here."

"But it's a trailer park."

"That's right. Center Grove Trailer Park. See that sign over there?"

Bromley looked and there it was sure enough: green letters on white background, CENTER GROVE TRAILER PARK.

"Huh," Bromley said, "I'll be damned. A trailer park."

Somehow he couldn't imagine Rex Stone living in a trailer. He had an odd thought: Did his horse Stormy live with him in there, too?

He paid the cabbie six bucks, six sweaty ones that had been deep in his summer pocket, and got out, lugging his big old Webcor recorder along with him.

The place was dusty, hot and Midwestern, a high sloping hill covered with long, modern trailers of the sort that put on the airs of a real house. Lying east and west, bracketing all the metal homes gleaming in the sunlight, were pastures, black and white dairy cows grazing, and distantly a farmer on a green John Deere raising plumes of dust as he did some tilling. A red Piper Cub circled lazily over head, like a papier mâché bird.

Each trailer had an address. Just like a house. He supposed he was being a snob, he after all lived in an apartment house, he after all lived in a three room apartment, but he couldn't help it. People who lived in trailers . . .

And then he remembered: his mother of course. "People

who live in trailers are hillbillies." She'd never offered any proof of this. That was not her way. She'd simply stated it so many times growing up that he'd come to believe it. At least a part of him had.

Hillbillies.

He found the trailer he was looking for. It was an Airstream, one of those silver jobs, and it looked to be a block long and it looked to be almost sinfully tidy as to shell and surrounding lawn. Indeed, bright chipper summer flowers had been planted all along the perimeter of the place. He wondered what his mother would make of that.

He went up and knocked and then there *he* was.

It was a strange feeling.

Here you'd spent all your life with an image of somebody fixed in your mind and then when you meet him—

Well, for him, Rex Stone would always be this tall, handsome, slender cuss in the literal white hat astride Stormy. His western clothes would have a discreet number of spangles, his hips would ride a pair of six guns always ready to impose justice on the lawless, and he'd just generally be—

—well, heroic. There was no other word for it. Heroic.

What he would not be was a) this old guy with a beer belly, wearing a t-shirt that said I'M AN OLD FART AND PROUD OF IT, b) this bald guy wearing a pair of lime green golf pants or c) this fat guy with a beer gut that looked a lot worse than Bromley's own.

"You Bromley?"

"Uh, yes."

"I'm Stone."

At least he had a strong grip. In fact, Bromley even winced a little.

Stone hadn't quite shut the door behind him. He said, "Be right back."

Not even inviting Bromley in or anything.

Bromley stood there listening to the noises of the trailer park: an obstinate lawn mower somewhere distant; a baby crying; a couple arguing and slamming more doors than you'd think a trailer could possibly hold; and a radio playing an aching country western ballad about heartbreak.

Bromley came back out. He carried two folded-up lawn chairs and a six pack of Hamms beer.

He didn't say anything, just nodded for Bromley to follow.

On the opposite end of the trailer was an overhang. Some tiles had been laid down to make a small patio. Here Stone flicked the chairs into proper position—his motions were young and powerful, belying his old fart appearance—and then he sat himself down and nodded for Bromley to do likewise.

"Beer?"

"Thanks," Bromley said. Actually, he didn't care much for alcohol but he wanted to be polite.

"That's an old one, isn't it?"

Bromley looked at his tape recorder. Indeed it was. A Webcor, a big heavy box with heads for reel-to-reel tape up top. Twenty-five years ago a friend of his had desperately needed money for some now forgotten reason. Bromley had paid him fifty dollars.

"It still works well, though. Just because it's old doesn't mean it can't do the job."

Stone laughed a slick Hollywood laugh and winked with great dramatic luridness. "That's what I tell the ladies about myself." Then he leaned forward and with a big powerful hand slapped the arm of Bromley's lawn chair. "Just because I'm old doesn't mean I can't do the job."

Bromley laughed, knowing he was expected to.

Stone seemed to relax some then, sitting back and sipping his beer. He studied Bromley for awhile and said, "Sorry, my friend."

"Sorry?"

"Sure. For being this old fart. You know, the way my t-shirt says."

"Well, heck, I—"

"Sure you did."

"I did?"

"Of course. You grew up seeing my movies and you've got this picture of me fixed in your head—this strong, handsome young man—and then you see me—" He shrugged. "I'm an old fart."

"No, you're not. You're—"

Stone waved a hand. "It doesn't bother me, son. It really doesn't. I mean, everybody gets old. Gene did and Roy did and Lash did—and now it's my turn."

Bromley wasn't sure why but he sort of liked it how Stone had called him "son." Made Bromley feel young somehow; as if most of his life (that great golden potential of youth) were still ahead of him and not mostly behind him.

"So you want to wind that puppy up?"

"That puppy?"

"The recorder. That big ole B-52 Webcor."

"Oh. Right. The recorder."

"And I'll tell you how it all started. And how it all ended."

"Yeah. Sure. Great."

So he wound that puppy up and Rex Stone started talking.

10

See, he'd never had any intention of being a movie star. He'd just been visiting in Los Angeles that day in 1934 when he was drinking a malt and having a ham sandwich in this drugstore when he happened to notice that, out on the sunny street, a group of people were standing there watching some kind of accident. Being naturally curious, and being from the Midwest and wanting to bring back all the great stories he could, he went outside to see what was going on, only it wasn't an accident, it was a movie, a bank robbery get-away was being staged, complete with a heart-stoppingly beautiful actress holding a tommy-gun and dangling an extra-long cigarette from her creamy red lips, and a fat bald little director who not only wore honest-to-God jodphurs but also carried a bullhorn and wore, if you could believe it, a monocle over his right eye.

That's how it started, how Presnell, that was the director, saw him standing there on the edge of the crowd, and between shots came over and started talking to him, and then had this very fetching young girl come over and take down his name and the address where he was staying, and four days—literally four days later—he was playing a six-line role in a western and singing as part of the cowboy singers who backed up the tone-deaf star.

Not that the rest of it came easy. It wasn't overnight or anything. By Stone's estimate he appeared in forty-seven movies (at least twenty of which came from Monogram, for God's sake) before it finally happened. One day Herbert Yates of Republic looked at sagging box office receipts for his westerns and then decided to give the singing cowboy movies one last try. Yates had been under the impression that singing cowboys had bit the dust about the time television started imposing itself on the American scene. Well, as usual, Herb's gut proved savvy: The Rex Stone pictures, eighteen of them in all, were the biggest-grossing Republic pictures of the era, and came in right behind Roy and Gene in overall grosses. Rex Stone was a star, at least in those small American burgs where the Fourth of July was still a big deal and where men, at least on occasion, still held doors for ladies.

As for Rex personally, he was not only a favorite with the kids, he was also a favorite with the starlets, as Louella

Parsons, then the country's premiere gossip columnist, noted with great delight. Rex was a big handsome lug and don't think he didn't take advantage of it. In one year he was hit with three fists (from jealous husbands), one champagne bottle (from a jealous fiancée) and two paternity suits. It was about then that he started marrying, a practice he kept up until the Rex Stone pictures started losing money and old Herb finally quit turning out westerns. Some movie historians had him marrying seven times; Rex himself claimed a mere five brides, though he did admit that there was one quickie Mexican marriage that might/ might not have been legal. Anyway, the marriages didn't exactly help his popularity. Roy and Gene scrupulously kept their private parts in their pants; Rex seemed to be flaunting his and in those areas of the country where the Fourth of July still meant something, and where men still opened doors for ladies, his rambunctious behavior with starlets hurt him, and hurt him badly.

Then came the fifties and all those failed TV pilots and TV series. He started looking heavier and older, and then he started flying to Italy where westerns were being turned out faster than pizzas, and where Rex Stone, even with something of a gut and something of a balding head, was still a big deal. Meanwhile, he kept on marrying, two brides between 1955 and 1959.

By now, the marriages were no longer scandals, they were jokes, the stuff of talk show repartee, and Rex Stone was pretty much finished.

Nobody heard from or about him. Various organizations such as The Cowboy Hall of Fame, which tried to keep members up on news of all the old film stars, did their best to track him down but even when he got the letters, he just tossed them away. He didn't want to go on the rodeo circuit and be this sad old chunky guy on this big golden Palomino waving his white Stetson to a crowd of kids who had no idea who he was. He did not want to cut ribbons at supermarket grand openings, he did not want to be surrounded by dozens of sad grotesque aging fans (no offense, Mr. Bromley) at "nostalgia" conventions, he did not want to be featured in every other fanzine about old western stars, and brag in print about how good movies had been back then and what shit (relatively speaking) they were today.

So for the past twenty obscure years, what he'd been doing was just moving around the country in his Airstream and living in all the places he'd always wanted to live (North Carolina for the beauty and the fishing; Arizona for the climate; New Hampshire for the beautiful autumns and New England sense of tradition and heritage.)

11

"Do you ever miss any of them?"

"Any of who?"

"You know, your wives."

"Oh."

"I mean, now that you're older and settled, isn't there one of them it would be nice to have along?"

At this point, Stone started glancing over his shoulder at the rear window.

Bromley hadn't noticed before, but despite the machine noise the air conditioning unit made, the back window was open about halfway. Bromley wondered why.

"Not really, I guess."

"You ever hear from any of them?"

"Uh, not really."

Then, unable to stop himself from asking this gushy question, Bromley said, "Wanda Mallory, was she as beautiful in person as she was on the screen?"

"She was a bitch and a gold-digger."

The thing was, Rex Stone hadn't said this. He'd just been sitting there holding his beer, with his mouth closed, and then out came the words.

Except the voice wasn't anything like Rex's at all. It was a crone's voice, a harsh cranky old lady's voice, and it had come wafting from the open back window.

Seeing how baffled Bromley looked, Stone said, "Why don't you try and get some sleep, Mother?" He was addressing the partially open rear window.

"You tell him what a little conniver she was. What a little conniver they all were."

"Did you take your medication this morning, Mother?"

"Don't try to change the subject. You tell him the truth about those little harlots."

"Yes, Mother."

"And I mean it."

"Yes, Mother."

"All that money you wasted on them."

"Yes, Mother."

"And I always had the smallest room. The very smallest room."

"Yes, Mother."

And then there was silence and Rex Stone just sat there sort of slumped over in his chair, whipped, beaten, this old man who looked as if some young guy had just delivered a killer blow to his solar plexus. He looked sad and embarrassed, and he even looked a little dazed and confused.

Bromley had no idea what to say.

The voice had reminded him a little of the mother's voice in *Psycho* whenever she got mad at Norman. Or actually (God forgive him) of his own mother's voice.

After awhile, still not looking Bromley straight in the eyes, Rex Stone said, "Why don't we hike on up to the rec room?

It's a real nice place." One thing: he was whispering his words.

Then he looked nervously up at the open rear window and then he started making these big pantomime gestures that said Follow Me.

Obviously Rex Stone, cowboy star, singer of lush romantic jukebox ballads, wooer and winner of untold gorgeous starlets, was scared shitless of his mom.

12

Ping.

"Every one of them?"

Pong.

"Every single god damn one of them."

Ping.

"But how?"

Pong.

"Because she got me by the throat the day I was born, and she hasn't let go since."

Ping.

They had been in the recreation hall for twenty minutes. It was a big and presently empty room shady and cool on this hot day, with two billiard tables, a jukebox, a candy machine, a Coke machine, a sign that said I'M A SQUARE DANCER AND PROUD OF IT, and the ping-pong table on which Bromley and Rex Stone had been playing for the past ten minutes. Stone was good at it; Bromley not.

"Hell, they even started whispering I was queer," Stone said. "Just married all these women to make things look good, you know, the way some of the actors did but hell, I like girls, not boys."

"So you loved every one?"

"Every single one."

"And your mother broke up each marriage?"

"Every single god damn one."

"You couldn't get rid of her?"

"Hell, I tried, don't think I didn't, but about the time my bride and I would move into our new place, my mother would come up with some new ailment and force me to let her move in."

"Is that what she meant by always having the smallest room?"

"Yup."

"So she's pretty much lived with you all your life?"

"All my life, ever since my father died anyway, when I was eighteen."

"And your wives—"

"They'd just get fed up with how she controlled me and then they'd—"

"—leave. They'd leave you. Right?" Bromley said, thinking of his own wife, and how much she'd resented his mother.

"That's exactly what they'd do. Leave."

Ping.

Pong.

The game went on.

And then Rex Stone said it, "You aren't going to put all this stuff about my mom in your article are you, son?"

There was a definite pleading tone in his voice and eyes now.

"No, I'd never do that, Mr. Stone."

"When the hell you going to start calling me Rex?" said the old man at the other end of the pool table.

Bromley smiled self-consciously. "All right—Rex."

"You think you got enough?"

"Yes; yes, I do." Bromley said, and he did, more than enough for a good article about Rex Stone. The fanzine readers would love it.

"You play pool?" Stone said.

"Better than I play ping-pong."

"Good. Then let's try a game."

They were each chalking their cues when the black phone on the west wall rang.

Rex glanced at it with genuine alarm.

He shook his head and walked over to it.

"Yes?"

He looked back at Bromley and shook his head. "All right, Mother, so you found me. Now what?"

Now he turned to the wall and muffled his voice, as if he didn't want Bromley to hear a word of it.

"You know how embarrassing this is?"

Pause.

"I'll go to the drug store tonight. Not right now, Mother."

Pause.

"I get pretty sick of you telling me that I don't take good care of you, Mother."

Pause.

"All right." And then a huge, sad sigh.

Rex Stone hung up and turned back to the phone.

"Maybe I'd better go check on her," he said. "Maybe she really is sick this time. You mind?"

"No, Rex, that's fine."

So they left the recreation hall and went back to the trailer. Nobody, not the little kids, not the mothers pushing strollers, seemed to pay any attention to Rex at all.

Bromley wanted to say: hey, this is *Rex Stone* for shit's sake! Rex Stone!

On the way back, Rex told him a couple of stories about Lash Larue and Tim Holt but Bromley could tell that Rex was still embarrassed about his mother's phone call.

Bromley said, "I'll have to be leaving in twenty minutes. There's only one more bus back to town today."

"I've really enjoyed this, son."

"So have I." And then Bromley decided to ask him. Rex would probably just say no, that it was a dumb idea, but what could it hurt to ask.

"Rex?"

"Yup."

"How would you feel about getting dressed up in your cowboy duds and having me take your photo?"

"Ah, hell, son, I don't know about that."

"It'd really go great with this article. Your fans would really appreciate it."

"You think they would?"

"I know they would. They'd love it."

So Rex Stone chewed it over for awhile and then shrugged and said, "How about just standing next to the Airstream?"

"That'd be great."

When they got back to the trailer, Rex started whispering again. "Why don't you wait out here, son. I'll go inside and change my clothes and then come back out. All right?"

"Fine."

So while Rex went inside, Bromley went over and got his Polaroid all ready.

Rex didn't come out in five minutes. Rex didn't come out in ten minutes. Rex didn't come out in fifteen minutes.

Bromley could hear it all, oh not all the words exactly, but certainly he heard the tone of voice. She was chewing on him in a steady stream of rancor that managed to stun and depress even Bromley, who wasn't even directly involved.

Every few minutes, he'd hear Rex say, "All right, Mother," in this really sad, resigned way.

And then it ended all of a sudden and the trailer door opened and there stood Rex Stone in his cowboy costume, the big white hat, the fancy cowboy clothes with spangles and fringes, the big six-guns slung low on his hips, and his trustworthy guitar dangling from his right hand.

Bromley hadn't realized till this moment just how old Rex Stone was.

How the whole face sagged into jowls.

How the whole gut swelled over the gunbelt.

How the hands were liver-spotted and trembling.

"I sure feel silly in this get-up, son," Rex said.

"But you look great."

"You sure about that?"

"I'm sure about that, Rex." Bromley waved his hand a little and said, "How about a step or two to the right, just to the side of the door."

And it was at that exact moment that the trailer door opened and out stepped a little kewpie-doll of a woman, no more than four-eight, four-nine, no more than eighty pounds, no more than two or three hundred years old, buried inside of some kind of gaudy pink K-Mart wrapper, her feet swathed in matching pink fluffy slippers that went *thwap, thwap, thwap* as she came down the stairs and took her place next to her son.

"I forgot to tell you," Rex Stone said, "Mom asked if she could be in the picture, too."

13

He tried for the next six weeks to write the article. Every few days, Rex would call and say, "Just wanted to see how it was going, son," and would then say, "You, uh, haven't mentioned my mom or anything in it, have you?" and Bromley would say, uh, no, Rex, I, uh, haven't.

But for some reason he couldn't write the piece.

Every time he started it, it was just too bleak. Here was a guy who'd been in a very real prison all his life. (Not unlike

Bromley.) Here was a guy who kept trying to break away and break away but couldn't. (Not unlike Bromley.) Here was a guy who had obviously wanted to spend his life with beautiful women but whose mother just didn't like the idea. (Not unlike Bromley.)

So how could you write a piece about a guy who'd been a hero to Bromley's whole generation . . . and tell the glum truth?

Because it was a pretty pathetic story.

14

Rex called two days after Bromley mailed him the article.

"Son," he said.

"Yes?"

"I—"

And then he made a familiar sound. "You know what that is, son?"

"You're blowing your nose?"

"Right. And you know why?"

"Why?"

"Because your article made me cry. And not cry for sad, son. Cry for happy."

"I'm glad you like it, Rex."

"I don't like it, son. I love it."

"I wasn't sure how you'd feel about it. I mean, I took certain liberties and I—"

"Son, you done good. You done real, real good."

15

The day the fanzine arrived, Bromley sat down in his re-cliner and started reading it, the way he did with all his own articles.

He turned back the cover and flipped through the pages till he saw the picture of Rex.

He'd stuck to the older photos. He certainly hadn't used the one with Rex's mother in it.

And then he read the caption under the photo of a young Rex as the cowboy star: "Here's a heartwarming article about cowboy film giant Rex Stone and how he's spent his life living on a horse ranch in Montana, sharing his bountiful life with his beautiful wife and three children."

Just the kind of life Bromley had always wished for himself.

A wife and three children.

Just the kind of life his generation would have expected Rex Stone to live.

16

"You haven't called me for a long time."

"I called you the night before last, Mother," Bromley said.

"I could be dead for all you care."

"Yes, Mother."

"Lying here on the floor while you're out running around."

"Yes, Mother."

And then he thought of Rex Stone's ranch in Montana, Rex and his beautiful starlet wife and their three perfectly behaved children.

He'd go visit Rex there someday soon.

Very soon.

That's just what he'd do.

"Are you listening to me?"

"Yes," Bromley said. "Yes, Mother, I always listen to you."

Someday very soon now.

On Roy Rogers

"You should have seen Elmer Kelton, Don Son-
nichsen, and others bidding against one another for
an autographed picture of Roy Rogers in Fort Worth
(the WWA convention). It went for something like
fifty dollars, outpulling everything autographed by
figures still living."
from a letter by Loren D. Estleman
to the author

He was never quite heroic, Roy wasn't, not in the way of
Gary Cooper or Randolph Scott, and maybe that's why we liked
him so much. He was sort of an older brother, and fallible in
the ways older brothers can sometimes be, and so even if he
didn't have a chiseled face or a mean eye, he was easier to like
and identify with than remote figures such as Coop or Randy.

Plus, he was a hell of a lot of fun.

A few weeks ago one of my favorite Rogers movies showed
up on the Christian Broadcasting Network, with Roy and Dale
introducing it and giving us show-biz anecdotes about how it
came to be made. The title of the film is *In Old Caliente* and it
contains all the usual singing-cowboy unlikelihoods and even
adds a few.

There is a scene where Roy and Gabby are imprisoned while
outside the bars a festive Spanish party goes on. What makes
Roy and Gabby's circumstances even worse is that in the
morning they are to be hung. By the neck. Until dead.

Now I don't know about you, but if that were to be my fate I'd probably be bitterly pacing off the size of my cell, cursing my captors and worrying about how to get out of there.

Not Roy. He sang a song. Not just a few bars but the whole thing. And it wasn't any Negro spiritual bemoaning the troubles-I've-seen. This was a Dick Powell musical type of number cast in the Tin Pan Alley Mexican mode. Roy, the night before he was to be hung, seemed to be having himself one hell of a good time.

What's remarkable about the Republic cycle of Rogers pictures is their style. Roy isn't a man's idea of a cowboy; he's a boy's idea of a cowboy and as such he works swell. He'd never crush a man's skull but he would dispatch him with a nice clean shot to the jaw; he'd never slip into any kind of paralyzing melancholy the way Coop sometimes seemed to—he'd take quick swift action; and he'd never lust after any of the dozens of beautiful Republic starlets but only desire them in the ways of western knighthood, doffing his fancy hat and "ma'am"ing them to death.

They hold up well today and maybe that's the most surprising thing of all, these films. The Rogers movies that were essentially crime movies still work as action pulp only a step or two down from *Black Mask* at its best and the western historicals are occasionally even superior to their Zane Grey origins, the Texas Ranger cycle being an exceptionally good fusion of history and Hollywood.

Then there was Gabby.

Even when I was five and six and seven I knew instinctively that Gabby Hayes was the Olivier of sidekicks and that all the Fuzzy St. Johns and Pat Buttrams were only clumsy imitators. The reason for Gabby's superiority was simple. He didn't do comedy. He did Mark Twain—the ultimate misanthrope. Gabby had two modes—pissing and moaning. Sometimes he pissed and moaned in the same sentence. Usually that involved "females" and what a shoddy imitation of real human beings they were.

Dale Evans, on the other hand, remains elusive even seen today. In some of the films, especially those in which she plays a rich Eastern girl come west to learn humility, she seems at moments almost as cranky as Gabby. But there was a gentle side to her, too, and in many of the production numbers where she sang and danced she was a genuine beauty of great poise and real talent.

Over the past twenty years several books have been published about western movies. Invariably, each takes its turn chastising the singing cowboys for being silly and inauthentic. In one book, the author goes into something resembling a seizure over how "gaudy" the costumes were.

But you know what? I don't give a damn about any of it. Roy and Dale and Gabby are good enough for any universe I ever inhabit. They appeared in some very good stories, the Sons of the Pioneers can still sing "Ghost Riders in the Sky" in a way that gives me chills, and any group of people who helped keep Roy Barcroft employed for three decades is all right with me.

People my age owe the Rogerses and Gabby (and, all right, Trigger, too) a debt we can't possibly repay because they're the sort of friends you take with you on into the cosmos, the Saturday afternoon B movies of the 1940s reverberating forever down the time lines.

Writing the Modern Western

A FEW YEARS AGO, enduring a party, I saw a former professor of mine. He told me how thrilled he was that I was writing mystery novels. "Ever considered any other kind of novel?" he asked.

"Yes," I said. "I've got a western coming out next month."

The professor looked as if I'd just confessed to burning down orphanages. "Shoot 'em ups, Ed?" he said. "You should stick to mysteries. They're a lot more respectable."

And so they are. In fact, nearly every genre is more respectable than the western.

But what foolish snobbery that is. Have you read or seen Larry McMurtry's *Lonesome Dove*? Or Jack Schaefer's *Shane*? Or Alan LeMay's *The Searchers*?

The fact is—and I would have told the professor this if he'd bothered to let me respond—the modern western is just as good, and many times better than, any other type of modern fiction. Unfortunately, not enough modern readers—or editors—know this yet.

But thanks to the efforts of half a dozen editors and perhaps half a hundred writers, America will know about its native fiction soon enough. The success of the TV mini-series *Lonesome Dove* inspired several publishers to begin publishing westerns for the first time in a decade or so.

But how about writing westerns? Is it a genre worth working in? Well, any genre that can call its own such contemporary authors as Brian Garfield, Elmore Leonard, Loren D. Estleman, Bill Pronzini and Joe Lansdale is certainly worth serious attention and serious work.

A few weeks ago a mystery writer of some note called me and asked if I'd help him plot his first western. I said I'd be glad to. I listened to him read three pages, and I stopped him. "This isn't a story," I said. "This is research." He made the same mistake I did when I first started working in the form. I forgot that the same human problems that drive all other fiction also drive westerns—hate, love, greed, vengeance, remorse. The western is a historical novel with the history secondary to the novel itself. An editor told me just yesterday, "I'm tired of seeing manuscripts that read like doctoral theses. First and foremost, I'm looking for a good story."

I got the idea for my own first western novel from a "60 Minutes" segment. The piece dealt with a California policeman who mistakenly shot to death a five-year-old boy while investigating what appeared to be a burglary. The policeman was undone by his act, ultimately quitting the force and spending a great deal of time in analysis.

As I watched this segment, another idea came to mind. A friend of mine who'd done two tours in Nam said that after he'd returned to the States permanently, he started going to confession, even though he wasn't Catholic. Confession helped him as nothing else seemed to.

At this time I was reading a history of famous western lawmen. I had just finished a chapter on bounty hunters. They were the pariahs of the frontier, despised equally by lawmen and outlaws alike.

My mind began to play with all these elements. What if you had a bounty hunter who acted honorably and what if this same bounty hunter, in the course of bringing in an outlaw, accidentally shot a young girl? What would become of the outlaw? My favorite western movie being Sam Peckinpah's *Ride the High Country*, I decided to make my main character, Leo Guild (like Randolph Scott and Joel McCrea in the film), in his fifties, a drifter and perpetually in need of work.

Over the next few days I wrote out sketches of his background, finally writing what I'd scribbled a few nights previous:

> The liveryman showed him several animals. When Guild saw the shave-tailed Appaloosa, he thought about the time he'd served a three-day sentence for assault and battery. He'd seen a drunken wrangler showing off for friends by trying to break a particularly troublesome stallion. Finally, the wrangler got so humiliated that he took out a knife and slashed the stallion's throat. Guild had gone over and kicked in three of the man's ribs and broken his nose. He had one of those tempers.

Guild came alive for me here—a lonely man more apt to identify with animals than people. I'm one of those types myself. Cats and dogs and horses have always struck me as infinitely preferable company to many of the people I've met.

The scene wasn't wholly from my imagination. If you take the task of writing western fiction seriously, you'll find yourself reading all sorts of oddball books. Before I began writing the first two Guild novels, for example, I spent forty or fifty hours in the library going through books on the historical midwest and west. I'd decided to put Guild in the Dakota Territory around the turn of the century. The idea of a bounty hunter functioning in a time when telephones and electric lights were becoming common had real appeal for me. My reading also gave me the scene with the wrangler and the stallion, an anecdote I picked up from the journals of a horseman who'd bought, sold, shown, and hunted horses all his life. He talked about how men treated their animals far better than they treated each other. And he talked about the most horrifying thing he'd ever seen—a drunken bronc buster slashing a horse's throat.

In writing the "Guild" books, I also did extensive research on *place*. In *Death Ground*, I have Guild reluctantly venture into the Badlands just at the start of a blizzard. I read Teddy Roosevelt's essay on the Badlands many times before I attempted the scene, and I also studied a book of photographs showing various angles of the land. I wanted the earth itself to play a dominant role:

> The plains before them resembled a white tundra with silver dust demons and a sudden moon gazing down on them like the callous eyes of a pitiless god. Everywhere you saw small black dots and knew they were animals— squirrels and raccoons and possums—that had frozen in the remorseless night. The only touch of ugly splendor anywhere was in the branches of the dead trees, silvered with ice and glinting like jewelry.

So there you have the two most important elements of the modern western—a strong human story and research used sparingly.

The third element is optional, but it's one I feel strongly about—theme. I like fiction that is *about* something. I believe that theme plays just as vital a part of storytelling as plot. For just one example, look at what Glendon Swarthout does in *The Shootist*: He has a dying man review his long and lonely life and try to make some sense of it.

Swarthout's novel is an exemplary modern western—its prose real poetry at times, its psychological portraiture so considered and wise that you feel decimated after finishing it.

So to my former professor, and to those of you who still think westerns equal shoot 'em ups, I wish you the happy experience of finding out otherwise.

A Bibliography of Books
by Ed Gorman

WESTERN NOVELS:

Guild. New York: M. Evans, 1986.
Death Ground. New York: M. Evans, 1987.
Blood Game. New York: M. Evans, 1988.
What the Dead Men Say. New York: M. Evans, 1990.
Dark Trail. New York: M. Evans, 1991.
Ride into Yesterday (as by Christopher Keegan). New York:
    Walker & Co., 1992.

HISTORICAL NOVELS:

Graves' Retreat. New York: Doubleday, 1989.
Night of Shadows. New York: Doubleday, 1990.

WESTERN ANTHOLOGY:

Westeryear. New York: M. Evans, 1988.

OTHER NOVELS:

Rough Cut. New York: St. Martin's Press, 1985.
New, Improved Murder. New York: St. Martin's Press, 1985.
Murder Straight Up. New York: St. Martin's Press, 1986.
Murder in the Wings. New York: St. Martin's Press, 1986.
Murder on the Aisle. New York: St. Martin's Press, 1987.

The Autumn Dead. New York: St. Martin's Press, 1987.

Several Deaths Later. New York: St. Martin's Press, 1988.

The Forsaken (as by Daniel Ransom). New York: St. Martin's Press, 1988.

A Cry of Shadows. New York: St. Martin's Press, 1990.

Night Kills. New York: Ballantine, 1991.

The Night Remembers. New York: St. Martin's Press, 1991.

The Long Midnight (as by Daniel Ransom). New York: Dell, 1992.

SHORT STORY COLLECTION:

Prisoners and Other Stories. Edgewood, Maryland: Chizmar Press, 1991.

Dark Whispers and Other Stories. Oregon: Pulphouse Publishing, 1992.

NONFICTION:

Jim Thompson: The Killers Inside Him (with Max Allan Collins). Cedar Rapids, Iowa: Fedora Press, 1983.

ANTHOLOGIES:

The Black Lizard Anthology of Crime Fiction. Berkeley, CA.: Creative Arts, 1987.

Mystery Scene Reader. Cedar Rapids, Iowa: Fedora Press, 1987.

The Second Black Lizard Anthology of Crime Fiction. Berkeley, CA.: Creative Arts, 1989.

Stalkers (with Martin H. Greenberg). Arlington Heights, Illinois: Dark Harvest, 1990.

Under the Gun (with Martin H. Greenberg & James Frenkel). New York: New American Library, 1990.

Dark Crimes. New York: Carroll & Graf, 1991.

Cat Crimes (with Martin H. Greenberg). New York: Donald I. Fine, 1991.

A Note about the Author

In a recent survey of suspense authors, the *San Diego Union* called Ed Gorman "One of today's best crime writers." Gorman has written such novels as *The Night Remembers* and *The Autumn Dead*. He has won the Shamus award and been nominated for both the Edgar and the Anthony awards.